D0114486

10 THINGS TO DO BEFORE I DIE

A Novel By
DANIEL EHRENHAFT

Delacorte Press

Published by
Delacorte Press
an imprint of
Random House Children's Books
a division of Random House, Inc.
New York

Copyright © 2004 by 17th Street Productions, an Alloy company.
Cover copyright © 2004 by 17th Street Productions.

All rights reserved. No part of this book may be reproduced or transmitted in any form or by any means, electronic or mechanical, including photocopying, recording, or by any information storage and retrieval system, without the written permission of the publisher, except where permitted by law.

The trademark Delacorte Press is registered in the U.S. Patent and Trademark Office and in other countries.

Produced by 17th Street Productions,
an Alloy company.
151 West 26th Street
New York, NY 10001

Visit us on the Web! www.randomhouse.com/teens

Educators and librarians, for a variety of teaching tools, visit us at
www.randomhouse.com/teachers

Library of Congress Cataloging-in-Publication Data

Ehrenhaft, Daniel.
   Ten things to do before I die / a novel by Daniel Ehrenhaft.
      p. cm.
   Summary: Just after his best friends make a list of things sixteen-year-old Ted should do to live it up, he learns that he has ingested poison and will be dead in twenty-four hours—which might be enough time to do everything on the list.
   ISBN 0-385-73007-1 (trade)—ISBN 0-385-90912-8 (library binding)
   [1. Terminally ill—Fiction. 2. Best friends—Fiction. 3. Friendship—Fiction. 4. Anxiety—Fiction. 5. New York (N.Y.)—Fiction.] I. Title.
   PZ7.E3235Te 2004
   [Fic]—dc22   2004006030

The text of this book is set in 10-point Avenir.

Book design by Christopher Grassi

Printed in the United States of America

November 2004

10 9 8 7 6 5 4 3

BVG

For Paulina and Georgia

Prologue: The Story of My Death

My name is Ted Burger. I am sixteen years old. I am an only child. I live in New York City.

I will not live to see seventeen.

What else? Let's see. . . . My voice is pretty deep but it squeaks sometimes, like an old rusty bicycle. I have curly brown hair. "Brillo pad hair," in my best friend Mark's words. I am tall and skinny. My fingers are, too. They look like twigs. "Musician's fingers," says my guitar teacher, Mr. Puccini. (Translation: "Girlie fingers.") I'm good at blowing stuff off. I have a hard time admitting certain things to myself. According to my parents, I have a "nutty, Borscht Belt sense of humor!" (I include the exclamation point because they tend to speak at a high-pitched volume.) What they mean is that I'm a third-rate clown, but they aren't really ones to talk.

This is the story of my death.

It starts the way all my stories do, as a bad joke whose tragic punch line somehow ends up signifying my whole life. Or death, in this case. Ha! Ha . . . ha . . . okay, maybe my parents are right. Maybe I am a clown. I don't have the greatest comic timing. I rarely instigate—bad things simply happen to me. Pie-in-the-face sorts of things. But don't just take my word for it. Consider the fortune I received on my sixteenth birthday (ironically, my last birthday ever, although I didn't know it at the time) when my parents took me to the Hong Phat Noodle House—and I swear I am not making this up:

> You will never have much of a future if you look
> for it in a cookie at a Chinese Restaurant. ☺

My mom's fortune promised a lifetime of infinite happiness. My dad's, a lifetime of wealth and fulfillment. When I complained to the waiter about mine, he told me that I should be pleased. "It's true, young man," he said with a smile. "One should never look for one's destiny in a dessert item. One should look for it in experience."

I agreed, sure—but deep down, I still felt sort of gypped. I asked for another one. He refused. Hong Phat policy is one fortune cookie per customer, period.

The real punch line is that I don't even like Chinese food all that much. I like french fries. But my parents forced me to go there because they said that I needed to learn how to use chopsticks. "It's a skill that will make you part of an important demographic, dear!" Mom insisted. That's a direct quote. To this day, I have no idea what she means. (I never learned how to use chopsticks, either.) My parents work together at the same advertising firm, so they talk a lot about stuff like "important demographics!" It's pretty much *all* they talk about. Maybe one day I will understand their baffling

DANiEL EHRENHAFT

pronouncements. I would if I weren't doomed to an early grave, that is.

Speaking of which, the story of my death also starts at a restaurant. It starts at the Circle Eat Diner with Mark and his girlfriend, Nikki. I can't imagine it starting any other way. Everything starts at the Circle Eat Diner with Mark and Nikki, at least everything that matters . . . everything that happens during those sublime, BS-filled hours when the three of us laugh and rant and eat, the hours just after school and before I have to run back home to Mom and Dad.

Okay, that's an exaggeration. I rarely have to run home to Mom and Dad. They aren't around very often. They take a lot of business trips. All of which is a long way of saying that I spend more time hanging out at the Circle Eat Diner with Mark and Nikki than I probably should.

Much more.

You'll see what I mean shortly. The story of my death has a very dramatic, pie-in-the-face beginning.

A Very Active Inner Life

Spring break has just started. No classes for a whole week! Woo-hoo! It's one of those rare gorgeous afternoons in Manhattan when the sky is swimming-pool blue and the breeze is crisp. There's no humidity at all.

Freedom! the day seems to shout. *Rock and roll!*

Well, the day might seem to shout that if I were outside. Inside the Circle Eat Diner, the day doesn't seem to shout anything. It stinks of grease. The three of us are huddled over the remnants of a burger, fries, and pickle. We pretty much order the same meal every time: Circle Eat #5, the Burger/Fries Combo. I eat the fries. Mark eats the burger. Nikki eats the pickle. The way Mark and Nikki are slouched across from me in the booth, they look more like a pair of models than a real-life couple—rail thin, dark, unblemished . . . poster children for the wonders of the #5 diet.

Mark's brown hair is a mess. His ratty T-shirt bears the logo GIVE THIS DAWG A BONE. His brown eyes are wild. They're always wild. This stems from a belief he's had since he was a little kid that something bizarre and miraculous could occur at any moment—a giant-squid attack, the Rapture—and when it does, it will require his personal involvement in some way. So he's perpetually on guard.

I envy him for this. I always have. He's never bored.

DANiEL EHRENHAFT

Nikki is hardly ever bored, either, but for less delusional reasons. She's got a very active inner life. This I can relate to. She's constantly turning everything over in her mind—every event and conversation, no matter how trivial—and milking it for its hidden wisdom. You can tell from the way she listens, from the way she looks you in the eye . . . you can even tell from how she dresses: mostly in black. With Nikki, blackness doesn't have an agenda. She isn't trying to play the role of a misunderstood hipster or a sullen goth. She isn't trying to fit in with any crowd, either. (To be honest, the three of us don't really belong to any crowd. Not unless you include the other people who hang out in the Circle Eat Diner all the time, like Old Meatloaf Lady and Guy with Crumbs in His Beard.) Nikki just doesn't put a whole lot of thought into her wardrobe. She's got too much else going on inside. Once she told me that the only reason she dresses in black is so her clothes will match her hair. I loved that.

Her eyes are what really tell the story, though. They're like onyx, calm to the point of being alien: the eyes of the extraterrestrials you see in UFO documentaries. They radiate that same mysterious, hypnotic "we-come-in-peace" vibe, even when she's joking around or scheming.

Funny: I probably think more than Nikki does about the way she looks. Ha! Not that I'd ever admit that to her. I definitely wouldn't admit it to Mark. I have a hard enough time admitting it to myself.

Wet Willy

Mark's fingers start to drum on our Formica tabletop. He's grinning. I can tell he's about to make a wisecrack. Sure enough, apropos of nothing, he says: "Dude, all you ever do is talk. Let's figure out something for you to *do* for once."

I haven't been talking. I haven't said a word in the last two minutes. I've been busy shoving soggy fries into my mouth. I know what he means, though.

"Like what?" I ask, playing along.

"How should I know, Burger? Something. Anything."

Mark has never called me by my first name. Not once. Not even when we first met back in the third grade, when our teacher, Ms. Bellevue, pulled me aside and introduced us. "Ted Burger, this is Mark Singer. Mark is an only child, too. Did you know that? You have something in common!" I didn't know what to say. Mark responded by licking his finger and sticking it my ear. The old wet Willy. "No, that's not appropriate!" Ms. Bellevue shrieked. She then sentenced him to a long time-out in the hall, after which Mark called me every permutation of Burger under the sun—Crapburger, Snotburger, Buttburger. . . .

The point being: even my own name can be used as a punch line. Most things can and always have been, especially in Mark's capable hands.

"How about if I start working here as a fry cook?" I suggest.

"I'm serious." Actually, I'm not, but Mark's accusation has provided a convenient excuse to segue into some juicy Circle Eat gossip. "I know they're looking for a new one. You know that guy Leo? He got fired."

"Leo got fired?" Nikki gasps. "The guy who looks like you?"

"He doesn't really look that much like me, does he?"

Nikki just smiles.

"Well, I'd say he rates about an eight on the Afro Q-Tip meter," Mark says. "You rate about a nine-point-five."

"Hey, I got the look, right? Why not flaunt it?"

Mark grins. "Amen, Burger. Amen."

Mark has told me a million times that I look like a Q-Tip with an extra-thick cotton swab at the top end—very skinny with "Brillo pad" hair. Personally, I believe Leo rates higher on the Afro Q-Tip meter than I do. Come to think of it, Mark himself rates the highest. But there's no point in arguing. Mark came up with the line first, so I can't throw it back at him. Besides, once you've been saddled with a disparaging product comparison, it's tough to shake.

"So when did Leo get fired?" Nikki presses.

"Last week," Mark says. "You didn't know?"

"I had no idea," she says. "We were here last week. Almost every day."

"Yeah, except Tuesday," he says. "That's when it happened. I heard it was crazy. I heard he was ranting about going on a killing spree."

"Are you serious?" Nikki glances toward the kitchen, her eyes widening. She lowers her voice and leans across the table. "But he's so nice."

"Yeah, well, you know what they say about 'nice.'" Mark makes air quotes with his greasy fingers.

"What do they say about 'nice'?" I ask.

"Pets are nice," he and Nikki chant in unison, as if reading from the same Hong Phat fortune cookie. "*People* are dogs."

I laugh. "I see. Did you guys hear that at an animal-rights rally?"

"My dad said it," Mark says. "He's looking for a 'thing.'"

"A thing?"

"That's what he said." He gobbles down some more of the burger.

"We were hanging out with Mark's dad the other night," Nikki explains. "He's been acting sort of sad lately. So I asked him what was wrong. He said that he doesn't have a 'thing'—you know, like a hobby or a passion or whatever. He said that he goes to work, he comes home and watches the news, blah, blah, blah. So Mark told him that maybe he should get a pet. You know, like a big furry dog, and they could play together, and go on long walks, and become best buddies. He thought this was really funny. He was like, 'I already have a crazy son. Isn't that enough?' And Mark was like, 'But pets are *nice*.' And he said, 'Son, you know, you're right. Pets *are* nice. People are dogs.'"

I glance at Mark. "Wow. Heavy. What did you say to that?"

He shrugs at me with his mouth half full and ketchup dribbling down his chin. "Woof, woof."

Things I Love About Rachel Klein

It's easy to see why Mark and Nikki make a great couple. For one, they look alike. They're both blessed with the same Mediterranean complexion, the same carefree thrift-store style. They've also nailed the elusive "we're-hot-and-we're-comfortable-with-it" vibe. They could be brother and sister. But it goes beyond just a physical resemblance. It's *metaphysical*. They're almost yin and yang. They share lots of private jokes and long, meaningful glances. They finish each other's sentences. They even hang out with each other's parents. It's as if they're adults.

I don't get it. Because my own girlfriend—

Let's just say that our relationship rests a few rungs lower on the maturity ladder.

It's not that I don't love Rachel Klein. Of course I love her. What's not to love? There's her blond hair (short cropped and funky), her blue eyes (soft), her fashion sense (bohemian: sandals and floral dresses), her GPA (4.0 and rising), her sense of social commitment (she's a member of Amnesty International), the fact that she's really—well, for lack of a better word—*nice* . . .

Yet . . . there are some things I don't love about Rachel Klein. In no particular order:

1. She thinks I have a crush on Nikki.
2. She bugs me about hanging out at the Circle Eat Diner so much. She once asked me—very, very nicely, of course: "Why spend all your time there with them when you could be spending time with me?"
3. She won't have sex until she's "ready."
4. See number 3.

The Swirling Vortex Inside My Head

Before I get back to the impending catastrophe at the diner, though, there's something I should mention. The only reason I was lucky enough to meet Rachel in the first place (and I know I was lucky) is because I approached her on a dare, instigated by Mark and Nikki. I wouldn't even have a girl-friend at all—much less one to complain about—if it weren't for them.

Here's what happened:

It was four months ago, the week before Thanksgiving break. Classes had just ended for the day. Mark and I were out loitering with the rest of the kids on the school's front stoop, shivering in the wind. We were waiting for Nikki.

DANIEL EHRENHAFT

Suddenly Mark spotted Rachel Klein.

"Burger, there's that new junior," he whispered. "You know, the Amnesty International chick? I saw her checking you out."

I was tempted to give Mark a wet Willy, but it would have been giving him too much credit. If he wanted to pull a prank, he had to tell a better lie than that.

"I'm serious, Burger," he said. "You should go up to her and introduce yourself."

"Are we being filmed for some sort of reality show right now?" I asked him dully.

"What do you mean?"

"I mean, you *are* trying to set me up for some kind of nationally televised humiliation, right?"

Mark scowled at me. "Dude, you gotta drop the clown act. It's getting old."

"Excuse me?"

"Why don't you believe that Rachel Klein would be inter-ested in you?"

"Gee, Mark, I don't know. Look at her. Now look at me. You do the math."

"The question you should be asking is: Why *wouldn't* she be interested in you?"

I offered a guess: "Because she's cute and I look like a Q-Tip with a Brillo pad Afro on top?"

"Burger," he moaned. "You're a stallion, dude! And who cares about looks, anyway? She obviously sees the swirling vortex inside your head. *That's* what matters."

"She sees the . . . what?"

"She sees that you're a tortured soul. She sees what the rest of them don't see, what I see. And what Nikki sees, too. She sees that you've got plans. She sees that you want something more . . . that you sit in your room alone and play guitar for hours—that, dude, you're a sick guitarist! She *sees* that. She sees that you worship that band from Brooklyn, Fakes the Clown—"

"Shakes the Clown. They're named after the movie."

"Whatever. She sees that you worship that band. But she sees that what you really should be doing is starting your own band, living life like the rock star you are—"

Out of nowhere Nikki's arms appeared around his waist. He hugged her back. As usual, their embrace had an oblivious, summer-blockbuster intensity; a passerby might think that Mark had just returned home from a long war or unlawful incarceration. Finally he took a deep breath.

"All I'm saying," he continued, "is that—"

"I should go up and introduce myself to Rachel Klein," I finished for him.

Mark smiled, satisfied. "Exactly."

"You mean that blond chick?" Nikki asked, letting him go.

DANIEL EHRENHAFT

"The new chick, right? The cute one? The one who's so into Amnesty International? That's so funny! I saw her checking Ted out in the cafeteria!"

"See?" Mark said. He beamed at me in triumph. "She's attracted to you, Burger. So what are you gonna do? I dare you to go up to her."

"I dare you, too," Nikki added. "It's about time you cashed in on your charm."

"My charm?"

"Yes, Ted," she said dryly. "That shy, mysterious, tortured-soul thing you work so hard to cover up with your clownish shenanigans? That charm?"

I didn't reply. Instead I just blushed, like the clown I am.

Something to Think About

Now, here's a question. Hypothetically, if you approach a pretty stranger on a foolish dare in order to escape a three's-a-crowd-type situation with your best friend and his girlfriend (a situation that arises all too often), are you also partly—secretly, unconsciously—motivated by a desire to *impress* your best friend's girlfriend?

You don't have to answer right now. It's just something to think about.

Exit Cue

Back at the Circle Eat, Mark has wiped our plate clean not only of hamburger, but also of grease. There's nothing left whatsoever. I can see my distorted reflection in the plate's ceramic white glaze. The guy's metabolism never ceases to amaze me. He's even taller than I am, he sucks up burgers with the efficiency of a vacuum cleaner—and he barely weighs in at a hundred twenty pounds.

"But seriously, Burger," he says. "What are you gonna do this spring break?"

"Well, I'm glad you asked," I tell him. "Because for once, I have a 'thing.' See, Rachel is helping to organize a big student Amnesty International retreat this summer in the Catskills. It's gonna be really fun. There are gonna be a bunch of kids from all over the country, hanging out at this old camp, and tons of speakers are going to come. Diplomats, ambassadors . . . it's the kind of thing that'll look awesome for colleges, you know? But I have to write an essay and fill out an application to get accepted. So Rachel is coming over tonight to help—"

"Whoa, slow down there, Chatty Cathy," Mark interrupts. "I don't know about this. You're saying you're going to spend the first night of spring break writing an essay?"

I smile. "Yes, Mark. Unlike you, I occasionally plan for the future."

"Yeah, but you're also telling me that filling out an application for a summer retreat, which will take you five minutes to finish, tops, counts as *doing* something? I don't think so." He adopts a pseudo-paternal tone. "And let's not forget that you really shouldn't go to the Catskills because your allergies will act up—"

"Don't listen to him," Nikki cuts in, elbowing Mark on the shoulder. "I think it's a great idea, Ted. It'll give you and Rachel a chance to spend some real time together, away from school, you know?"

"So how come you've never invited me on a retreat, then?" Mark asks her.

"Because you can't sit still." She frowns at him. "And wipe your face, for God's sake. You're disgusting."

"Oh, sorry," Mark says.

He winks at me, then reaches below the table and pulls Nikki's jean jacket out of her bag, using the sleeve to clean the ketchup off his chin. But Nikki just winks at me, too, then wipes the ketchup-stained jacket back on Mark's face. Mark laughs. Nikki doesn't. I recognize my exit cue.

"Later, dogs," I say, scooting out of the booth.

"Wait!" Mark whispers. He grabs one of my knapsack straps, reining me in. "Check it out!"

My shoulders sag. "Come on, man." I groan. "I gotta go. Anyway, I don't feel so well." It's true. My stomach is churning. Sometimes the fries at the Circle Eat don't go down as smoothly as they should. This particular nausea is worse than usual. It's actually making me a little dizzy.

"Sit *down*," Mark hisses, forcing me back into the seat with a violent yank.

"What's the problem?" I ask.

He jerks a thumb toward the register. He looks panicked.

Then I see why: that other high scorer on the Afro Q-Tip meter, the recently fired Leo, has just walked in. He's lurking by the door. And there's definitely something . . . well, a little *off* about him. His face is a gruesome white, except for the purple sacks under his eyes. His Brillo pad hair is a mess. He's also wearing a ratty black overcoat. It looks as if it's come straight out of a Dumpster. This is conspicuous because Leo never wears an overcoat, not even when it's cold outside—which it isn't. Leo wears a blue parka. (At least, as far as I know. And I *know*, having eaten his fries almost every single weekday afternoon for the past two years.) Furthermore, Leo is now glaring at the balding young Greek guy, Greg, who works the front counter.

Not that any of this really grabs my attention.

No, what grabs my attention is how Leo has now jammed his right hand into his right coat-pocket. Something pointy is protruding from the fabric. This pointy thing is slowly being aimed straight at Greg—

"Everybody freeze!" Leo shrieks. "I want to ask you something! Do you know that *fired* is just *fried*, misspelled?"

DANiEL EHRENHAFT

Sniveling Coward

Every cliché is well founded. When you're face to face with death, your life really does flash before your eyes. I guess it's a lot more enjoyable to relive the past than it is to confront a deranged fry cook with a concealed gun.

So while some brave souls may try to jump in and save the day, others—namely sniveling cowards like Ted Burger—freeze up.

My brain hops the next train out of the station. I start thinking about Rachel. I realize that Rachel will never have sex with me no matter how "ready" she is because I'll be dead. Not unless she's into necrophilia. Ha! Ha . . . no, that's not funny, either. It's not even shameful. It's despicable. But still, I think about all the mistakes I made with her, about how I should have appreciated her more—and thankfully (or not), Mark slams the brakes on this sad train of thought by jumping out of our booth and lunging at Leo.

A Round of Waters for Everyone!

"Mark!" Nikki shrieks in horror. "Don't!"

But Mark is already in midair.

I can't believe it. I mean, I can; this is Mark, after all—*He's going to get killed. My best friend is going to get killed.*

I gaze, slack jawed, as he hurtles down the aisle.

Leo seems as perplexed as the rest of us. His purple-ringed eyes narrow into slits. Oddly, though, he doesn't move. So Mark crashes into him. The impact is a blur of black fabric. Mark's T-shirt and Leo's ratty overcoat meld into one. They topple to the floor. Instinctively I leap to my feet. I watch as they wrestle. It's not like the wrestling you see on TV. It's not choreographed. It's sloppy and awkward, and they slip on the linoleum and grunt and . . . at this point I'm having difficulty breathing. I'm also having heart palpitations. Plus my stomach feels as if it's being ground up in a Dispose-All.

I don't want to start spring break like this, I frantically think. *I want to start spring break by laughing and telling jokes*—I know I should dive in there and interfere, and aid my best friend in his struggle, but I can't. I'm paralyzed.

Somehow Mark pins him.

"Yes!" I shout.

Leo tries to squirm. He's beefier than Mark is, but Mark's skinny limbs are stronger than they appear. He exploits the temporary advantage by shoving his hand into Leo's overcoat. *No, no, no. Don't do that. That's how accidents happen.*

I hold my breath. Mark pulls out the gun and sticks it into Leo's face, and . . .

"Oh my God," Nikki whispers.

Wait a second. Wait just a second here.

DANiEL EHRENHAFT

The gun is green.

Translucent green. It's made of plastic.

It's a water gun.

Mark scowls at it. "What the—"

"Suckers!" Leo screams.

He flips Mark over and bolts for the exit. A second later the door slams behind him. He disappears down Seventh Avenue.

I glance at Nikki.

A shaky smile spreads across her face.

We both turn to Mark. He's still lying flat on his back on the floor.

Then slowly, very slowly, he starts to laugh.

It's over, I say to myself, fighting to catch my breath. *It's all over.*

In a flash Mark is scrambling to his feet and waving the water gun over his head. He squirts it a few times into the air— his sweaty face ecstatic, his black T-shirt soaked—and cries, "A round of waters for everyone!"

Several customers sigh. A few burst into applause. I nearly collapse.

Mark performs a silly little dance in front of us all. I tumble back into the vinyl seat, as exhausted and triumphant as if I'd been the hero myself. Although there is a prickling in my belly, a little warning flash that maybe Mark *didn't* quite save us from this twisted freak, that maybe this is only the start of something much more sinister . . .

But I have an overactive imagination. It *is* over. Yes. Of course it is. I should know better.

That prickling is probably just Leo's last batch of fries.

Opportunity

Several long, nervous minutes go by before the Circle Eat Diner begins to settle down. In the meantime everybody decides to leave except Mark, Nikki, and me. And a funny thing happens. All the regulars take turns patting Mark on the back on their way out. None of us has ever actually communicated beyond "hi" until now. But the brief crisis has united us, made us a family. It's like a receiving line at a bar mitzvah.

"Nice work, sport," says Old Meatloaf Lady.

"You've got guts, kid!" says Guy with Crumbs in His Beard.

"Word, G.," says P.Y.T. (Pale Young Thug, so christened because he has a machine gun tattoo on his bluish white forearm and several names crossed out under it).

Mark shrugs and thanks each one graciously.

I want to be part of this mass exodus, too. I want to pat Mark on the back and congratulate him and then get the hell out. I'm quivering and dry mouthed. Also, something is wrong with my stomach. It's not just prickling anymore. It's gurgling. But I can't leave. Mark is in no hurry. He insists on staying.

DANiEL EHRENHAFT

And I can't blame him. Not only is he decompressing after an extremely traumatic experience (he disarmed an insane criminal, for God's sake), Nikki is also smothering him with affection and gratitude. Which he deserves. So I don't want to spoil the moment.

Still, I'm very relieved when Greg, the balding Greek guy behind the counter, announces: "I'm gonna call the goddamn cops. I don't want that pecker coming back in here and scaring all my customers away."

"Sounds good," I reply. I stand up.

"Hey!" Nikki cries, letting go of Mark. "Where do you think you're going?"

"I'm gonna split, too," I say. "Just until the cops arrive and clear this up. Anyway, I should go home and get ready to meet Rachel."

"You have plenty of time," Mark says. "What is there to clear up? It was a water gun. The guy's a nutcase." He pauses. "Which is too bad because he was an awesome fry cook."

"Not that awesome." I groan.

"Listen, Burger, you want to know something?"

"Can I know it later?"

"I'm being serious!" he yells. "You know why I went after Leo? Why I really did it? To teach you a lesson, dude! To show you what it's like to grab life by the *cajones*! To lead by example!"

In spite of the nausea, I almost laugh. That might just be the silliest lie he's ever told. Even Nikki rolls her eyes. I know exactly why he went after Leo: for no other reason than that he's an impulsive maniac. But I also know now that I have no choice but to stay. If I bolt, he'll chase me down. This is classic Mark: he's pumped full of adrenaline—rightly so—eager to talk, and capable of anything. So I collapse back into the vinyl seat. I owe him that much. He did try to save my life.

"Look, here's the deal," he says earnestly. "It's the first day of spring break. Your parents are out of town until tomorrow night, right?"

"How did you know that?"

"You told me, Burger, remember? The way I see it, you should use today and tomorrow as if they were your last days on earth. You should try going crazy for once. Like I just did. You should try taking some risks, you know what I mean? Have you ever really taken a risk before?"

"I introduced myself to Rachel Klein, didn't I?" I answer. It's the only risk I can think of.

"Okay, aside from that," Mark says. "What I'm saying is: Have you ever really *lived*, Burger?"

I blink at him. Interesting question. It reminds me of that Hong Phat fortune cookie. I probably should have tried to bolt. I hate it when people ask me stuff like this. Especially Mark. I can hardly think of anything that makes me more

DANiEL EHRENHAFT

uncomfortable. Except . . . oh, I don't know. Acting like a coward, maybe?

The Hands of a Burly Lumberjack

"I propose we make a list," Mark announces. He's still sweaty
and manic. He pulls a napkin from the aluminum dispenser on
the table and then unzips my knapsack, fumbling through it. "I
propose we make a list of the things Burger should do over the
next twenty-four hours. Okay? Let's make a list of ten things. Like
the Ten Commandments. You know, just to make it official?" He
finds a ballpoint pen and clicks it open. "So. Number one . . ."

Nikki smiles at me. "How about losing his virginity?"

Mark brightens. "Excellent!" He leans over the napkin and
writes:

Burger's Spring Break
1. Lose virginity.

My face heats up like a burner. It's bright red. *How does
Nikki know that I'm a virgin?* Actually, that's an incredibly stupid
question. Of course she knows that I'm a virgin. She knows
everything about me. She's in love with my best friend.

I grab my knapsack. "Okay, you guys. I'll see you later—"

"No, no, no," Nikki says, clamping her palm down on my wrist. "I'm sorry. That was so lame of me. Forget I said that."

"It's all right," I mumble.

Even under duress, I can't help noticing how much softer Nikki's hands are than Rachel's. Aside from the silver rings (one on every finger), Nikki's hands are like velvet. Rachel's hands are hard and calloused. There's a good reason for this: she volunteers three days a week tending to a community garden in Harlem—something that I admire even more than her commitment to Amnesty International, something that most kids our age would never *think* to do—but . . . well, the downside is that all the hours of weeding and digging have given her the hands of a burly lumberjack.

"But Ted, you know, the first day of spring break is pretty romantic," Nikki points out. "I mean, you were planning on seeing Rachel tonight anyway, right? It's the perfect time to do it." She gives my arm an affectionate squeeze, the kind a nanny might give, then lets go. "I should know."

Mark glances up at her, his brow furrowed. "We didn't do it for the first time on the first day of spring break."

"Yeah, we did," she says.

"No, I remember," Mark says. "It was the second day."

She shakes her head, confused. "We—" All at once she smiles demurely. "Oh, yeah. You're right."

"You think I'd get that date wrong?" Mark mutters, smiling back.

DANIEL EHRENHAFT

I can tell that they aren't being dense. They aren't trying to make me feel awkward, either. They're just lost in their own reveries, thinking out loud in front of their fifth wheel—the poor clown whom they're trying to help—because Nikki honestly couldn't remember the exact day she lost her virginity.

And it gets worse.

Together they run down their strategy for me:

1. I should finish the Amnesty International application before Rachel comes and meets me this afternoon. Then she'll be thrilled.

2. No, actually, I should blow her off and ask her to meet me later tonight because then she'll get annoyed.

3. Which means, of course, she'll be that much *more* thrilled when she sees that it was all a big surprise for her benefit. It will also give me time to finish the application *and* to turn the Burger apartment into a full-fledged love nest: candles, incense, maybe some red wine from my parents' liquor cabinet, groovy seventies music.

4. Yeah, the whole atmosphere will be pure aphrodisiac. . . .

5. And then Rachel and I will talk like we've never talked because I'll have finished the application on my own . . . and it'll prove that I truly want to be with her, that I want to go away with her this summer, that we should be together—

Mark stiffens.

"What?" Nikki asks.

He turns to me, his face creased in concern. "Burger, can you get into your parents' liquor cabinet?"

"What are you talking about?"

"Do your parents keep the liquor cabinet locked?"

"Don't know. Never tried to open it. I'll have to get back to you on that one."

Mark flashes Nikki an inscrutable look.

She nods, reading the message, whatever it is.

"The wine conundrum," she says.

"Hmmm . . ." Mark pauses mysteriously and chews on the ballpoint for a few moments. "Well, it'll be much better if it happens without booze anyway." He leans over the napkin, back in business mode. "Next?"

Hooked on the Drug of Flattery

The real conundrum has nothing to do with access to my parents' liquor cabinet, obviously. The real conundrum is that Rachel has told me a dozen times that she won't have sex until she's "ready."

Well, not precisely a dozen times. She's told me nine times—the exact number of times we've made out. The pattern is always the same, too. I ask to kiss her; she says yes; I get

DANiEL EHRENHAFT

frisky; she backs off. "I'm sorry, but I just can't go any farther, Ted," she whispers sweetly, in a voice that's like a cold shower, like an ice pick through my chest. It's a pattern that dates back to the first time we ever hooked up, in fact.

I'll always remember that day very, very clearly.

It was just before Christmas break, about a month after we first met. A Wednesday afternoon. We were alone in her apartment, sitting on her bed. Rachel's room is a very mellow place to hang out. There's lots of psychedelic art and a Lava lamp on her desk. Her paisley bedspread is made of "100% recycled fabric." She was trying to play the Beatles' "Day Tripper" on her acoustic guitar. I was grinning stupidly, trying not to stare at her cleavage. We hadn't so much as held hands at this point.

I mention these details because they cut to the very heart of our relationship.

You see, when I first walked up to Rachel on Mark and Nikki's dare, I found out that they were right: Rachel *had* been checking me out. But not for the reasons Mark and Nikki thought. It seemed she and I shared the same guitar teacher, Mr. Puccini. Rachel said she'd been hoping to meet me because Mr. Puccini claimed I was his prize student. She needed someone to help tune her battered six-string. "I'm so glad you introduced yourself!" she told me. "Would you mind giving me a hand with the tuning?"

Needless to say, I felt like pinching myself. I'd been expecting her to ignore me or tell me to get lost. Instead she was inviting me over to her apartment.

That same day, though, I learned she was telling the truth. If I didn't help her tune her guitar, it produced the same kind of flatulent noises you would generally associate with ant-squashing or with pipes that are about to burst. Worse, she didn't seem to notice. So after that, we started hanging out a lot. I felt I owed it to her. I forsook the Circle Eat almost every day to go to her apartment. Still, it was weird . . . our conversation was always wry and flirtatious, but we never talked about anything other than guitar tuning. Were we friends? I wasn't sure. But if we weren't friends, then what were we?

On the other hand, I discovered we shared the same fundamental flaw. We both craved the validation of others. We *bled* for it. So in a way, we made the perfect pair. Two addicts, hooked on the drug of flattery. I bombarded her with phony compliments: "Rachel, you're really getting great at tuning that thing!" In turn, she obliged me with phony adulation: "I can't believe how talented you are!" It felt so good. I'd never heard a line like this before, not from any girl, anyway. Not from Mark, either, disregarding his "sick guitarist" comment. And forget about my parents. Honestly, I don't know if they'd ever even listened to me play or tune the guitar—I mean *listened,* with their ears—aside from yelling at me to put it down so I could come watch an important commercial.

But something changed that day in her bedroom.

"Maybe I should just take up the harmonica," Rachel joked. (It was abundantly clear that she would never master "Day Tripper," no matter how many years she put into it.) "I mean, you're working so hard showing me all this stuff, and I'm still not getting anywhere." She bent over and gently placed the guitar back in its case. "Christmas is right around the corner. I could donate my guitar to that secondhand shop—"

"Rachel, you *can't* give up," I cut in. "You're making a lot of progress. You're great for a beginner. You know that."

"I don't know, Ted. You're always so nice. . . ." She scooted closer on the mattress, so close that our butts were practically touching. "You know what my problem is? I don't have the passion you have. I need to find music that I'm really passionate about. Like you did."

"Uh . . . what do you mean?"

"You're passionate about that band," she said.

"That band?" I repeated inanely. My voice squeaked. Our noses were eight inches apart. Suddenly I was fighting to ignore two simultaneous crises—the first being that I'd never seen Rachel's face in all its wide-open beautiful perfection, down to the tiny pores above her nostrils, the second being that my heart was about to explode.

"You know, that band from Brooklyn?" she said. "Snakes the Clown?"

"Shakes the Clown. See, they're named after this movie that—"

"Yeah, but what I want to know is: What was it about them that inspired you? What was it about them that made you so passionate about music? That turned you into this incredible guitar player?"

I blushed. "Rachel, I'm not that good."

"Yes, you are." She patted me on the thigh. Her hand lingered.

With that one little gesture, something inside me snapped. I'm not sure why. But I started jabbering about Shakes the Clown. About how they're a joke band but *not*, because they're amazing musicians. About how I first discovered them by accident, as I was channel surfing. About how I skimmed past a local cable-access show called *Bad Manners*, but I had to go back because I glimpsed an off-kilter trio . . . so off-kilter that I thought I was hallucinating—two scrawny white guys in matching prison overalls (barely older than me!) plus a huge black woman with a massive Afro on drums—and they were playing a deranged acoustic Black-Sabbath-meets-bluegrass cover of "I Am Woman, Hear Me Roar" . . . or they were, until the singer-guitarist, Hip E. Shake (I didn't even know his moniker then), stopped the band midsong and asked cryptically: "How can I start a war if I have no beer?"—then walked off, ending the performance.

Words gushed from my mouth like a froth of exploding toilet water.

I stopped listening to myself. I was conscious only of Rachel's attentive eyes. I gazed into that sea of gorgeous blue. I realized that I must have been desperate to share my love of Shakes the Clown with *someone* because nobody else seemed to care about it.

But Rachel Klein did. Rachel Klein was my ideal woman.

I leaned forward and kissed her.

She flinched. Her face turned pink.

"Ted!" she gasped.

The moment came to a terrible, screeching halt. *I just made a move on Rachel Klein. While talking about Shakes the Clown! What was I thinking? I wasn't thinking. Oh God. OH GOD! That was the stupidest—*

"Don't you ask permission?" she murmured.

I blinked a few times. I wasn't sure if I'd heard her correctly. "Permission?"

"Don't you ask a girl permission before you kiss her?"

"I . . . uh . . ."

"You can kiss me, just so you know." She smiled shyly. "But in the future, just ask my permission, okay?"

I couldn't answer. I'd lost the ability to form words. Luckily it didn't matter. Before I could nod or even grunt, she pounced on me.

And what ensued—

It was great, of course. It defied description. (Well, I *could* describe it, but personally I think that getting into the nitty-gritty of a fervent make-out session is in poor taste.) Yet at the same time, I was a little sad. I couldn't help glimpsing the future.

It's true. I saw it all. I saw how things would change between us. I saw the end of the Guitar Tuning Flirtation. I saw that if I had to ask permission every time I wanted to kiss her, I'd want to hide from that—hide in anxiety and embarrassment—so I'd start making up lame excuses to avoid Rachel whenever I could, despite everything else I liked about her. I'd start hanging out at the Circle Eat Diner again. I'd hang out there more than ever. Yes, I'd slink back to the very place where I spent so much time daydreaming about *having* a girlfriend, and I saw that my life would come full circle . . . and maybe I even saw myself sitting there with Mark and Nikki on that glorious first day of spring break, knowing that Rachel would never, ever, grant me permission to lose my virginity to her, no matter what.

That Dickhead, Billy Rifkin

"Look, man, I'm really not feeling well," I mumble to Mark. "I have to split."

"Five more minutes, Burger," he insists.

I shake my head and clutch my belly. Maybe it was the near-death experience or maybe it was Leo's last batch of fries, but I'm on the verge of barfing.

"Two more minutes," Nikki bargains, seizing my arm again.

"We'll speed up," Mark promises. He leans over the napkin. "So, after you've taken care of business . . ."

2. Jam with Shakes the Clown

"Of course!" Nikki cries. "You're a genius, sweetie! Ted, you're their number one fan. They practically *know* you."

"Well, actually, I'm just on their mailing list. A thousand people are on their mailing list. Probably more. But—"

"Whatever." Nikki waves her hands. "The thing is, we should figure out a way for you to meet them. Or better yet, play for them! You know? So you can blow them away with your guitar!"

"We should do even better than that," Mark says. "We *will* do better than that."

He wriggles his eyebrows and scribbles down task number three in such large, bold letters that I can read it upside down across the table:

3. *PARTY* with Shakes the Clown

"Now, that's what I'm talking about, Burger!" he shouts. "Partying like a rock star!" He slams his fist on the Formica, rattling the plate and silverware.

Nikki nods at me. There's a strange, wistful sparkle in her

eyes. It looks as if a tear might fall, as if she's thinking: *Oh, our little Teddy is going to party like a rock star. I'm so proud.*

Ironically, I'm getting a little teary, too—but only because my allergies have started to act up. This is puzzling. My allergies (dog hair, cat hair, et cetera) never bother me inside the climate-controlled, grease-saturated environment of the Circle Eat Diner. All right. Something is definitely wrong with me. My body is protesting for some reason. Maybe it's an aftershock from the Leo incident. Maybe it's some sort of psychosomatic reaction. Whatever the reason, the discomfort has migrated from my stomach to my sinuses. I have to go home. As soon as possible. ASAP, as my parents like to say. As in: "Ted, put that guitar down and get in here ay-sap!"

"What's the matter, Ted?" Nikki asks.

"Mmm," I groan. "Not . . . feeling . . . well. I really—"

"I got it!" Mark cries. Then he grins. "Number four. Revenge!"

"Revenge?"

"Burger, you gotta get back at that dickhead, Billy Rifkin!" he yells at me. "Remember Billy Rifkin? That punk skate-rat? The dwarf with the mop-top haircut? Remember in the sixth grade when he stole your guitar strings out of your knapsack? And you couldn't prove it because he threw the strings in the sewer, and everyone laughed at you? Remember?"

Yes, I remember—but why bring it up? I shoot a quick glance at Nikki. This is one Ted Burger anecdote she doesn't need to hear.

DANiEL EHRENHAFT

Mark's elation just as suddenly fades. "Damn. There's only one problem." He chews on my ballpoint. "I don't know where Billy Rifkin lives or goes to school or anything. He switched schools after sixth grade. But whatever. You'll track him down."

And do what? I wonder. *Barf on him?*

"Hey, Mark, maybe we should let Ted go," Nikki says.

She's eyeing me now with genuine concern. This time there's nothing maternal or nannyish about it. It's more the concern of someone who's face to face with a volcano that's about to erupt. She starts pushing away from me in her seat, mashing her back into the vinyl.

"But I'm on a roll," Mark says. "It's all coming together!" He chuckles. "I promise you, Burger: this is gonna be the *sickest* spring break of your life. This spring break is gonna be *ill*—"

"Don't say those words," I moan.

Mark stares at me. But it's too late. He's already triggered some sort of reaction inside my intestinal tract. *Bad, bad, bad.* Now is the time to leave. No doubt about it. I gather what little strength I have. For once I have to follow Mark's advice and get off my butt and do something. I grab my knapsack and hightail it out of the booth— dizzy, half blind, and with my stomach on the verge of exploding.

"Burger, wait!" he shouts.

His hand clamps down my shoulder.

Uh-oh. My head swoops down fast. My eyes are blurry. I feel as if I'm on a roller coaster. I cover my mouth.

Mark spins me around to face him.

"Burger, listen, I only—" He breaks off. "Wow, you're really pale. Jeez. Maybe you should call a doctor." Then he brightens. "Oh, hey, I forgot to tell you! My dad just got a job at St. Vincent's. He's going to be the administrator of the pediatric—"

"Mark, I don't feel so well," I croak.

He responds with a typical easygoing laugh. "Okay, okay. I'm sorry. But hey, at least take the napkin." He shoves it into my knapsack. "And don't lose it. I'm serious. We're only up to number four. Besides, you know what they say. You know what they say, Burger, don't you?"

He escorts me to the door and opens it, accompanying me onto the sidewalk. I can feel the fries swimming up toward my throat. . . .

"The best ideas are always written on a napkin," he concludes.

And with that, I puke.

Twenty Bucks

No need to go into the gory details, obviously.

But once I escape—after apologizing to Mark for nearly throwing up on his sneakers, after promising him that yes, I'm fine, so he should just go back inside . . . after thanking him again for saving our lives (true, technically it was only a water gun, but none of us knew) . . . after lurching away from him with vomit on my T-shirt . . . after all that, the full impact of Mark's last words hits me.

"The best ideas are always written on a napkin."

You see . . .

Often I refer to my parents as "out-of-their-gourds wacko." Sometimes even to their faces. You might think that this is kind of harsh. After all, everyone's parents are wacko in a way. Just look at Mark's dad, with his obsession about having a "thing." Wackoness comes in a zillion different colors. The mere fact that my parents say everything with an implied exclamation point isn't all that wacko. Nor is the fact that they occasionally nag me to stop playing guitar to watch an "important commercial!" That's just typical parent stuff. (Sort of.) Even taking into consideration that every square inch of our apartment is smothered in framed photos of us and every single person we've ever met (I'll get to this later), . . . you still might ask: What's so wacko about that?

Good question. Nothing is really so wacko about that.

But at the end of this past summer, the day before school started, the following scene occurred. (Note: What you are about to witness is entirely true. No artistic liberties have been taken. I only describe it in screenplay format because it provides me with the sniveling detachment I need to cope with it.)

INT—BURGER FAMILY STUDY—DAY

TED, a 16-year-old boy who rates a nine-point-five on the Afro Q-Tip meter, stands anxiously behind **MOM** and **DAD,** two forty-eight-year-olds in matching nylon sweat suits. Mom, a classic mother-in-advertising—expensive hairdo, slender build, deep wrinkles around her lips and eyes from the perma-smile—sits at a desk, typing on a laptop. Dad, a Distinguished Gray, sits next to her. He stares at the screen. Neither is aware that their only child is in the room.

                    TED

   Hey, you guys? Sorry to interrupt, but can I have, like, twenty bucks? I really need to go shopping for school supplies.

                    MOM

Ted! I'm sorry we've been so busy.

                    TED

It's okay, Mom. But I just—

DANiEL EHRENHAFT

MOM

Funny you bring up school supplies! Did you know that your father and I are doing the ad campaign for a school-supply company? We're going on their corporate retreat next week.

TED

Yeah, you told me. Right now, though, I just really need to buy a notebook and some pens and stuff. School starts tomorrow.

Dad whirls around to Ted, grinning.

DAD

Don't worry. You don't need a notebook this year.

TED

I don't?

DAD

No. We've got you covered, kiddo! You need the Napkin.

                              TED

I need the . . . what?

                              DAD

The Napkin! It's the latest digital organizer
from the Y-Guys Company. Better than a PalmPilot,
better than a notebook . . . it's the ultimate
high school study aid. No more wasting paper, no
more worrying about your pens running out of
ink—it fits into your jeans pocket, just like a
napkin. And for safety's sake, its memory can be
backed up on any Mac or PC—

                              TED

Actually, I do sort of need a notebook, Dad.
Okay?

                              DAD

I don't think so, Ted. Wait until you hear
what the ad slogan is. Or better yet, try to
guess! Go on!

                              TED

Do I have to?

DAD

You're really gonna love it. You'll see.

TED

Can I guess after I get the twenty bucks?

DAD

Honey, should we tell him?

Mom finally stops typing. She turns and beams at me.

MOM AND DAD *(in unison)*

"The best ideas are always written on a Napkin™!"

They burst into laughter. Ted storms over and snatches Dad's wallet out of his sweatpants pocket. Dad doesn't seem to notice. He and Mom gaze proudly into each other's eyes, laughing away. Ted removes a twenty-dollar bill and drops the wallet on the floor.

FADE OUT

Now do you understand why I think they're so out-of-their-gourds wacko?

Anyway, back to the story of my death:

The nausea subsides as I continue hobbling down Seventh Avenue toward my apartment. The burning in my eyes subsides as well. Apparently I've escaped whatever unseen animal hair is floating around the Circle Eat.

It's still a gorgeous day, too. It's literally picture perfect, the kind of afternoon they use in commercials to promote tourism in New York. The sun is just starting to sink toward the Village, a golden ball hovering over the water towers and town house roofs. The traffic isn't so bad yet, either. There's hardly any honking or yelling.

That's the good news.

The bad news is that I'm still about a mile away from home. I'm only crossing Seventeenth Street, and we live on Barrow Street— on the top floor of a renovated brownstone just west of Seventh Avenue. So even if I hop on the subway, I doubt I'll get there any faster. It's only two stops. Plus I'll be trapped underground.

The *worse* news is that although I'm no longer queasy, I feel as if somebody is repeatedly jabbing my abdomen with a white-hot fire iron. I'm still dizzy, too. I've also noticed a high-pitched ringing in my left ear. It sounds like amplifier feedback.

All of which tells me that whatever sickness my body tried to barf out back at the diner hasn't quite left me yet.

But I'm not worried. Being the glass-half-full kind of guy that I am, I know that I'm not in any serious danger. After all, even if I were to collapse face-first in the intersection (I'm presently staggering across Sixteenth and Seventh), St. Vincent's Hospital is only four blocks away—hey, that reminds me! Mark's dad just got a job there . . . he's the new hospital administrator of . . . what? Something! Doesn't matter! I bet if I go right now, he can make sure that I see a doctor ASAP!

"Ay-sap!"

Crimes Against Humanity

Six minutes later I'm standing in front of a bulletproof window, desperately trying to convince a four-hundred-pound, rayon-clad security guard that I'm not insane.

"I'm telling you, he works here," I repeat as patiently as I can. "Mr. Joshua Singer. He's my best friend's father. He's an administrator."

The security guard glares at me from deep within the folds of his pasty face. His skin is the color of a fast-food egg breakfast.

"I'm telling *you*, kid," he growls. "We have no record of a Joshua Singer at this hospital. Not as an administrator, not as a doctor, not as a nurse, not as an intern. Not even as a patient.

Understand? Now if you want to see a doctor, go to the emergency room and wait with everybody else—"

"But I—"

"Next?" he shouts.

I slither away from the line that's beginning to form behind me. Unlike Seventh Avenue, the traffic in this hospital is stuck in a serious jam—and the sunlight is no longer tourism-commercial perfect. No, the way it's streaming through the floor-to-ceiling windows somehow makes the hustle and bustle that much more confusing. The longer I stand there, the more everything is thrown into jumbled disarray: the institutional tile, the sad-sack visitors, the doctors with their clipboards . . . all of it grotesquely lit by this horrible, slanted, dizzying glare. . . .

I have to get out of here before I get sick again.

The glass is no longer half full. Not even close. It's not even half empty. It's dishwasher clean. I stagger back toward the exit. Odd: my head feels as if it's revolving like a radar dish on an ocean liner, like one of those whirligig towers that pirouette relentlessly, around and around, spinning and spinning and—

"Can I help you?"

I look up. I realize I've been doubled over. I'm also clutching my ears in a vain effort to drown out the peculiar wailing screech that nobody else seems to hear. But now I'm saved. Saved! Because the young woman who asked this extraordinarily considerate question—this beautiful *doctor* (she has to be a doctor; she's wearing green hospital scrubs), this gorgeous nerd with the thick glasses and ponytail—she wants to help me!

"Yes, please, thank you," I gasp.

"What's the matter? Is it your ears?"

"No. I mean, yes, but not totally. My ears are only part of it. I feel really dizzy. There's a pain in my side. I just threw up. And I hear this weird ringing—wait a second. Actually, you know what? It's starting to die down a little. But it was really loud there for a bit."

She gives me a quick once-over. Her eyebrows are tightly knit behind the Coke bottle lenses. She sniffs loudly.

"What is it?" I ask.

Without a word, she takes my elbow and escorts me to a more private spot at the end of the hall. We pause next to a big, fake palm tree.

"Have you been drinking?" she whispers.

I frown. "Excuse me?"

"I have to ask," she says.

"No!" I bark.

She flashes an apologetic grin. "Okay, okay, I believe you. Let me ask you something else: Have you eaten anything unusual recently?"

I hesitate for a moment. "Just some fries. But I eat fries every day of the week, pretty much."

"Oh, I see." She laughs. "Very healthy."

Maybe she's trying to be overly friendly now to compensate for the drinking accusation, but I relax a little. I admit: I'm a sucker for the attention of a female, *any* female. What sixteen-year-old isn't?

"Well, not *every* day," I say sheepishly.

"Do you notice if the ringing is louder in one ear?"

"I . . . louder in one ear?" It strikes me as an odd question, but she's the doctor. I concentrate for a moment. "Yeah. I think it is. I think it's louder in my right ear."

"I see," she says. She scans my entire body again, pausing briefly at the vomit stains on my T-shirt. There's zero emotion involved. She studies me the way a butcher might study a spoiled side of beef. *Any meat worth saving on this carcass?* she's asking herself. Or so I imagine. She chews a nail. "I think you should wait here."

"Why?"

All of a sudden she grins again. "I'd like a doctor to take a look at you," she answers, a little too cheerfully. "I'll go see if one's available."

"You're not a doctor?"

She laughs. "No, I'm just an intern. Don't worry!"

Until she brought it up, I *wasn't* worried. Now I feel a shudder of fear creeping up my spine. "Why should I worry?"

"You shouldn't."

"Okay."

"How old are you?" she asks.

"Sixteen," I tell her.

Her smile falters.

"What?" I say, alarmed. "Is that a problem?"

She forces another laugh, peering through the sunlight toward a bank of elevators. "Of course not. Listen, why don't you call one or both of your parents and tell them to meet you here? I'll be right back. Okay?"

Alarm turns to full-fledged panic. "My parents? Why do I have to call them? They're on a business trip. What's going on? I really—"

"Shhh," she whispers. She casts a furtive glance back toward the security guard, then lays a hand on my shoulder and puts another phony smile on her face. "If we're going to conduct any kind of examination procedure, we need the consent of a parent or guardian. You know, for X-rays and stuff. Or maybe minor surgery. Okay?"

Minor surgery? What are you, nuts? No! It's not okay! Not in the least!

That's what I'd like to tell her. But I'm too frightened. Because that phrase, that one phrase, is stuck in my brain for all time. I'm talking about the phrase that instantly conjures a thousand different visions of twisted hospital horror movies and sadistic torture and crimes against humanity—the crimes that Rachel works so hard to prevent as a member of our school's chapter of Amnesty International, that go way beyond minor surgery. . . .

"*Examination procedure.*"

Everyone knows about phrases like that. Evil geniuses use phrases like that. Maniacal dictators. Movie villains. They use them to cover up awful truths.

"I'll be right back," the intern is saying.

"Huh? No! Where are you going?"

"To find a doctor." She hurries toward the elevators. "We might as well rule some things out, right? I'll be right back. Call your parents, okay, sweetheart?"

The Creeps

No way am I waiting around for her to find a doctor.

For one thing, hospitals give me the creeps. Not just because "examination procedures" are performed here and "things" need to be "ruled out." It's the whole atmosphere: the blinding sunlight, the stale air, the miserable patients with the massive bandages on their arms (because blood has just been drawn)—not to mention that every single bench and cafeteria and pediatric wing is "Memorial" *this* and "In Honor of" *that,* so there's this unseen shroud of death hanging over the whole place—

Wait.

For no reason whatsoever, I suddenly realize why the security guard was such a jerk to me. Mark's father just *got* the job as an administrator here. So he hasn't started. His name isn't in the computer. He's not an employee yet.

Which means he can't help me.

But that's not even the issue. The real issue is that even if I did call my parents (which I have no intention of doing), they can't help me, either. They're in Denver at a billboard convention. They're a good two-thousand miles away.

I catch a glimpse of the intern's ponytail as it swishes into one of the elevators.

The doors close behind her.

My eyes zero in on a glowing sign nearby:

Cardiology: 2

Transplant: 2

Radiology: 3

The list goes on. The sign is also illustrated with those universal stick figures that represent all humanity: Mr. and Mrs. Public Toilet—a triangle skirt for her, a blank formless body for him. Except here the couple don't just provide helpful directions to the nearest bathroom. No, here they're stricken with terrible diseases and injuries. Mrs. Public Toilet has to go to the ER. Mr. Public Toilet is due for chemotherapy. The prognosis is not good for either of them. *Okay*. I've seen enough. Time to split. I know exactly what Glasses and Ponytail has in mind for me. It's not just X-rays. She's thinking stomach pumping, invasive surgery—that's what she meant when she said "examination procedures." She wasn't talking about checking my pulse or sticking a thermometer in my mouth. You don't need a doctor or your parents' consent for *that*.

And all I did was throw up! So I have some ringing in my ears. So I'm dizzy. What's the big deal?

The truth is, I have no desire to find out what's really wrong with me. Maybe that's a character flaw. But that's who I am. We all have problems. I just don't care to know what my particular problems are.

Once again I've been given my exit cue. And this time, thank God, Mark and Nikki aren't around to stop me.

Lou and Frankie

Ahhh.

It's good to be outside. What with the sunset, the cool breeze . . . yes, remarkably, by the time I round the corner onto Barrow Street, I feel better. Or close enough. I'm no longer hobbling. The fire iron in my abdomen has cooled from white-hot to lukewarm. My head is revolving less like a radar dish and more like an abandoned merry-go-round, slowly decelerating to a natural standstill. I'm fine! Sure. Of course I am. I've just suffered some weird, inexplicable affliction. That's all. Stuff like this happens all the time in New York City. There is nothing that needs to be "ruled out." No . . .

Rachel?

She's standing in front of my brownstone.

Our eyes meet.

Mine are pink and puffy. Hers are ice blue. They're the same color the sky was an hour ago—*Whoops.* It occurs to me that I was supposed to be home an hour ago. I was supposed to call her on her cell phone.

But why is she here?

I glance at my watch. It's not even five-thirty. Usually she's up at the community garden in Harlem *until* five-thirty. I was supposed to call her at five so we could confirm our date for six so she could help me with the Amnesty International Summer Retreat application.

"Hey, Ted!" she cries, waving.

She hurries toward me. Right away I see that she must have skipped Harlem altogether, because she's not in her gardening clothes. She's wearing a black flower-print dress and a gray button-down sweater. And sandals. Her short blond hair is mussed from the breeze. Her green knapsack dangles from her left shoulder. She looks really gorgeous, actually—especially in the sunset. But I have to admit: I just don't want to see her right now. Not until I've changed out of my smelly T-shirt.

"So where have you been?" she asks. "I thought you were gonna be here to call me. I wanted to surprise you."

"I, uh, see, I wasn't feeling well, so I—"

"Oh my God." Her eyes zero in on the vomit stains. "Have you been *drinking*?"

I start to laugh.

Her soft features melt in distress.

Whoops again. "Of course not!" I exclaim. Inexplicably, I sound guilty. So I laugh harder. It doesn't help. "But it's so funny you ask that because this nurse—"

"Your face is all bloated," she interrupts. "Your eyes are bloodshot."

The laughter stops. "Yeah, because I'm sick."

She shakes her head. "Oh, Ted . . . you *are* drunk. I know what guys look like when they get drunk. I have two older brothers, remember? Hockey players?"

I swallow. Sure, I remember: Lou and Frankie. The twins. How could I forget? They're twenty years old, violent, and built like refrigerators. They aren't my biggest fans, either. The one time I met them, they called me Forrest Chump. I doubt if they even know my real name. And they're home from college for spring break, which means they're probably bored and looking for some action—like, say, pummeling

DANIEL EHRENHAFT

their sister's clownish boyfriend because he got "drunk" and blew her off.

"I bet I know what happened," Rachel mumbles. She stares at her feet. "I bet Mark and Nikki roped you into getting drunk with them after school, right? Because it's the first day of spring break and all? And since you have a crush on Nikki, you went along with them."

"Rachel, come on! Do you know how ridiculous that is? Do you even know what just happened to me? I was practically shot."

She pauses. "Shot?"

"Well, not technically. I mean, it was only a water gun. But still, it was—"

"A water gun?" If I saw a flicker of forgiveness in her eyes, it's gone.

"Well, you sort of had to be there. It would take too long to explain. The point is I'm not drunk and I *don't* have a crush on Nikki. I went to the diner with her and Mark, just like I told you I was going to do. Then Leo, this crazy fry-cook . . . See, he burst in and threatened to kill us, and then Mark tackled him, and then I started feeling sick. So I stopped by St. Vincent's. That's why I'm late."

Rachel just stares at me. Finally she shakes her head again.

"That's the best lie you can come up with?" she whispers. "It doesn't even make any sense, Ted."

"Ted, what's wrong?" Rachel asks me pointedly. "I mean, really?"

I shrug. "I just don't feel well."

"Well, then, I should go, right?"

"No, Rachel, don't go. I'm sorry. Come upstairs."

"Why? You're drunk."

For a terrible second I almost make a stupid wisecrack. I almost say, "Okay, so maybe you should get drunk, too." But I don't.

Unfortunately, I do start thinking . . .

What would happen if we actually *did* get drunk?

I could break into my parents' liquor cabinet, per Mark's suggestion. I could pour us some wine. I could dim the lights. I could put on Mom and Dad's *Feel the Love, 1975!* compilation CD. (The liner notes: *Not Sold in Any Store! All Hits by the Original Recording Artists!*) The music is soft and funky—and just cheesy enough to be romantic. The CD cover is brilliant, too: a fuzzy ski-lodge-style photo of a seventies couple by a fireplace on a bearskin rug, gazing into each other's eyes and drinking from crystal goblets. The man is tanned and swarthy, like a pirate. Thick hair blankets his open-shirted chest. The woman is skinny, blond, and bug-eyed. She's wearing an oversized lime green turtleneck. The fat collar hangs down over her puny bust

DANIEL EHRENHAFT

like a sexy polyester necklace. I could suggest to Rachel that we dress up exactly like the couple in the photo, and drink wine, and pretend that we're feeling the love, circa 1975—

"Ted?" Rachel says.

"Huh?"

"Is this funny to you?"

"Is what funny?"

"You're smiling. Have you heard a word I've said?"

"Yes!" I lie, too emphatically. "Of course I have. It's just . . . I want to lie down."

She sighs. "You know, Ted, you've got problems."

"I agree."

"It's this avoidance thing," she says. "It really bums me out. Whenever you don't want to deal with something, you just run away."

I'm not sure how to respond. She has a point.

"You didn't want to deal with the Amnesty retreat application, right?" she asks. "So you blew it off to hang out with your friends and get drunk. Which is fine. I mean, it's the first day of spring break. But that's not the sad part. The sad part is that you thought you could fool me. The sad part is that you assumed I'd be up at the garden until six. You assumed you had time to come back here and clean yourself up. But you want to know something, Ted?" Her voice catches; she sounds as if she's about to cry. "You want to know why I'm not up there? I canceled today to *surprise* you. Those people up there were counting on me to help them, and I canceled because I knew this application was a chore for you, and so I . . . oh, forget it."

"Rachel, no, wait. What?"

She heads off toward the subway entrance on the corner. "Nothing," she mutters. She doesn't turn around. "But you don't have to make up some BS excuse about getting held up by a fry cook with a water gun."

"It's true!" I call after her.

Now I feel bad. I feel *worse* than bad. I was wrong; I didn't want to get into a fight. I hate fighting. Besides, who would want to fight with Rachel? She's too nice! And it's completely my fault: I baited her into an argument when I should have been grateful for her showing up here to surprise me. I should have taken time to explain the truth instead of spacing out with a vision of drunkenly reenacting *Feel the Love, 1975!*

For a second I wonder if I should chase after her. Probably not a wise move. The dizziness has kicked in again. The sidewalk appears to be tilting for some reason.

"Rachel, I'm sorry—"

She hurries down the subway steps.

Good grief. Now I know I should chase after her. I know this with every fiber of my guilty soul. I should be honest. I should explain what happened: that I just lost myself for a second in one of those wild daydreams I always have whenever I want to be somewhere else—the daydreams that won't come true but that still give me the little pick-me-ups I need to get through the unpleasant moments in life. . . .

But I don't.

I never do what I should.

The Most Billboards per Square Mile of Any Town in the World

I can't dwell on Rachel, I tell myself. No. Right now I have to figure out why I feel so sick. Then I can lie down. And after that, I can call her and apologize. Rachel and I both need a chance to cool off, anyway. So as soon as I finish all the tasks that require my immediate attention—changing the T-shirt, washing the face, brushing the teeth—I'm ready to get started.

Except . . .

I find myself standing in my darkened bedroom, staring at my phone.

Which is when I think: I don't really want to know what's wrong with me. Of course I don't. It'll freak me out too much.

It's a little past 6 p.m.

I have one new message. The numeral 1 blinks in red on the digital panel, over and over again.

In addition to taking me to the Hong Phat Noodle House on my sixteenth birthday, my parents also gave me a private phone line. Plus a celly, a TV, a cable modem, and a credit card. "Tools for adulthood!" they said. It was generous loot, to be sure, but it was sort of overwhelming. I didn't really need those tools for adulthood. I was happy using theirs. But now the issue never even comes up. Now, on those rare occasions when they're actually home, there's no reason to bug them about getting off the phone or the Net or watching what I want to watch on TV. Likewise, they don't have to bug me. They can tune in to the Home Shopping Network to their hearts' content. In fact, we barely have to communicate at all. Which is . . . good?

Blink blink blink . . .

Maybe it's Rachel. Maybe she beat me to an apology. That would certainly be in keeping with her character: to take the blame for something that isn't her fault at all just to avoid conflict. So I hope it isn't Rachel. *Be strong!* I urge her, attempting to communicate telepathically via my vertiginous brain. *You should be mad at me!*

As I gaze at the red flash, I'm conscious of two things. The first is that according to Mark and Nikki, I'm supposed to have sex with Rachel tonight. Approximate odds of that happening: four zillion to one. The second is that the phone has begun to tilt to the left. So has the messy desk on which it sits. And the messy floor on which the desk sits. Everything is tilting. Just like the sidewalk outside. Also, I haven't turned on the lights yet.

The entire tilting room is cloaked in eerie bluish shadows. I'm about to lose my balance.

I stumble into the desk chair and jab a finger at the answering machine button.

"You have one new message," the automated female voice pleasantly announces. "Message one received today, 4:12 p.m."

Beep!

"Hi, Ted!"

It's Dad. His voice blasts from the speaker, full of tinny enthusiasm: "How's it going? How's that application coming along? Remember our agreement. You finish it ay-sap, all right? Then you can have some fun. How's the weather there? The weather here in Denver is just fantastic!"

"Well, *I* don't know how the weather is," Mom cuts in. For once she doesn't include an exclamation point. She sounds grumpy. "I was stuck inside the Hyatt all day. I will say that the convention floor does have great air-conditioning. Your father and I did the B-to-B ads for the wholesaler."

Dad laughs. "Yes, your mother had to work the convention floor, but I got the day off. You'll never guess where I went! There's a small town in Colorado that has the most billboards per square mile of any—"

"Not the most billboards," Mom interrupts.

"Yes, the most per square mile. Of any town in the whole world."

"It has a lot, dear. But not the most."

"It was in *The Guinness Book*," Dad tells her brusquely.

Mom sniffs. "You're just making this up."

"I'm not! You weren't there! I saw a billboard for it! It was—"

I slam my hand down on the machine.

"Your message has been erased," the automated voice concludes, as pleasantly as ever. "End of messages."

Two Out of Four Ain't Bad

So, everybody of importance in my life has been accounted for. My parents have touched base to update me about their exciting business trip. My blameless girlfriend has stormed off in a huff. Mark and Nikki are most likely still at the diner, celebrating Mark's triumphant heroism. All of which means I have some much-needed time to myself. *Now* I can figure out what's wrong with me.

I bury my cowardice and turn on the computer.

The screen spins in circles, like vinyl on a turntable.

I don't get it. I know it isn't spinning. So why does it look that way? I grit my teeth, fighting to ignore the hallucination as I punch the words *dizziness nausea ringing in the ears abdomen pain* into a "Feeling Lucky?" search engine. Several sites appear. All of them revolve (literally) around something called Ménière's disease.

I click on the first one.

DO YOU HAVE MÉNIÈRE'S DISEASE?
IF YOU SUFFER FROM SOME OR ALL
OF THE FOLLOWING SYMPTOMS,
THE ANSWER COULD BE YES:

1. Frequent episodes of severe rotary vertigo or dizziness
2. Progressive low-frequency hearing loss
3. Tinnitus
4. Pressure in the ears

Number one, check.

Number two, not so much. I hear fine. Except I hear ringing, too.

Number three . . . *What the—?*

I grab a dictionary. My breath quickens. Words like this make me nervous, even more nervous than words like *examination procedure*. I riffle through the pages, frantic. At least I know what those words mean. But I have no idea about—

tin-ni-tus *n. med.* Ringing in the ears.

Oh.

I toss the dictionary on the floor.

Number three, check.

Number four . . . I don't think so. Nope. No pressure.

That leaves me with two out of four of the symptoms. Fifty percent. I sense I've failed some sort of test. Still, two out of four ain't bad. "Some or all," right? I skim through the rest of the medical literature on the site, searching for any indication that Ménière's disease is fatal. There is none. I do learn, however, that it leaves its victims incapacitated for hours on end with nightmarish head spins and vomiting. The gist seems to be that Ménière's doesn't kill you but that death might be preferable once you get it. And there's something else: it almost never strikes anybody under the age of thirty.

I lean back in the chair. *Hmmm.*

Once again, the trusty Internet has raised a lot more questions than it has answered.

Do I have this awful disease? Could I be one of those one-in-a-million victims in the under-thirty crowd? Or maybe even the first? Is it one of the "things" that the intern wanted to "rule out"? Is that why she needed parental consent for a . . . whatever?

Actually, I know who can solve all these riddles. He's the reason I went to St. Vincent's in the first place. I glance at my watch. It's already six-fifteen. He's definitely home by now. He never gets home past six. He likes to have a beer and watch the news. (He might not want to admit it, but that *is* his

DANiEL EHRENHAFT

"thing.") Mark even joins him sometimes. He's just a phone call away.

I dial the number faster than I've ever dialed it before.

A Very Grim Confluence of Conversations

"Hello?"

"Hey, Mr. Singer. It's—"

"Burger! How are you?"

"Well, actually . . ."

"Your buddy Mark isn't home right now. He's out with Nikki."

"Yeah, I know. I wanted to talk to you."

"Me?" Mr. Singer laughs. "Why? What did Mark do this time? Try to buy me a dog?"

"No, um . . . I have a medical question."

He sighs. I can hear the TV in the background. I probably should have waited until the news was over. Oh, well. It's too late now. Besides, I'm desperate.

"I'm not a doctor, Burger, remember?" Mr. Singer tells me. He's told me this many times before, and we both know it. "I'm a hospital administrator."

"But you've given me good advice in the past," I point out. (It's true. When I was twelve, he correctly diagnosed me with a stomach virus that my parents believed was appendicitis.) "I was just wondering: Is it possible that I have Ménière's disease?"

"Ménière's disease?" He laughs again and takes a swig of beer. "You know, Burger, I always pegged you as a clown but never as a hypochondriac. But in answer to your question, no. Well, yes, it's *possible,* but very unlikely. What are your symptoms?"

"I feel like the room is spinning. I have a weird ache in my side. I have tinnitus."

"Tinnitus, huh?" He takes another long pull from the bottle. "Big word."

"I looked it up."

"Hey, I'm sorry, Burger. I've just been sort of grouchy lately. I don't mean to be supercilious."

Super-what? I eye the dictionary on the floor, but it's too far away.

"Let me ask you something," he says. "Is the ringing louder in one ear?"

"Yes! It's louder in my right ear! The intern at St. Vincent's asked me the exact same thing. Oh, congratulations on your new job there, by the way."

"Thanks. But wait, you say you were at St. Vincent's? And they didn't tell you what was wrong?"

"No, see, the intern went to look for a doctor, and she told me to call my parents for consent, but I *can't* call my parents—I mean, I can call them, but they can't come give consent because they're in Denver—so I just . . . um, I sort of left."

Silence.

"Mr. Singer?"

"I'm here. Sorry." He doesn't sound so grouchy anymore. "Listen, Ted, I think you should go back there."

Ted? I swallow. The Singers don't call me Ted. Well, Mrs. Singer does, but she and Mr. Singer got divorced six years ago, and she moved to Florida—so I hardly ever see her. Mr. Singer calls me Burger. Like his son does. *Ted* is bad. *Ted* is a no-no. Mr. Singer would only call me Ted if he knew something was wrong.

"Why should I go back there?" I ask.

"Hey, come on, don't worry!" he says with a big laugh. (That same fake laughter the intern gave me.) "Just go get checked out. I'm sure it's nothing. And by the way, your parents don't have to be present to give consent. They can do it over the phone. But if you can't get in touch with them, I'd be happy to do it."

I glance at the computer screen. It whirls like a pinwheel. Now that the sun has set, its dead white glow provides the only light in the room. "If it's nothing, why do I have to deal with it now?" I'm having difficulty catching my breath. "Why can't I just wait until my parents get back?"

"I'm sure the hospital just wants to rule some things out."

"That's exactly what the intern said!" I gasp.

"Right," he confirms with utter calm. "They just want to perform a couple of examination procedures. . . ." His voice trails off for a moment. "Hey, are you watching the news right now?"

"No. Why?"

"Something happened at that diner you guys always go to. You know, the one on Seventh Avenue? The Circle Eat?"

The spinning computer screen freezes before my eyes. "What?"

"Yeah, it's on channel two. Are you near a TV? You should really check this out. It's live. . . . It looks like there are tons of cops there. Wait. They're hauling some guy away. Hey! He looks a little like you—"

BZZZT!

It's the front door buzzer.

"Ted?"

"I gotta go," I mutter. "I'm sorry, Mr. Singer. Thanks. Bye."

I hang up.

BZZZT! BZZZT! BZZZZT!

The buzzing is very insistent. It has an odd effect: it turns my limbs to gelatin. A thought has occurred to me. Yes, as I sit in that dark, terrible bedroom (practically a tomb!), a horrid worst-case scenario has materialized: Leo ran off to get a real gun. And then he returned to the diner to shoot Mark. And now the cops have come here to tell me that my best friend—

DANiEL EHRENHAFT

BZZZT!

"Whoa!"

Vertigo sends me toppling to the floor.

Ouch.

I bang my side. It's cool, though. I'm coping. For the first time ever—despite my condition—I'm confronting trauma head-on. I stagger down the hall and through the pitch-black living room into the foyer, collapsing against the Talk button.

"Hello?" I whisper.

"Burger!"

Thank God. It's Mark's voice, blaring from the white plastic speaker. But it's so distorted I can barely understand him.

"Dude, we have to talk!" he says. "It's Mark and Nikki! You're in trouble!"

Trouble? I stand there, numb and frozen.

"Burger? You there?"

I lift a shaky arm and press the button again. "Yeah, Mark, I'm here."

"You have to let us up, dude. Now! I don't want to freak you out, but see, Leo really flipped his lid—and—and—"

Mark is stammering. He never stammers. I'm the one who stammers.

"Leo poisoned the fries!" Nikki wails. "You've been poisoned, Ted! You've been *poisoned*!"

Epiphany

I surprise myself.

I'm super-relaxed. I'm beyond super-relaxed. I'm Zen-like. I'm pretty sure I know why, too. Denial is the first stage of "the five stages of grief." (Or so my psych teacher taught me.) The great thing is, knowing I'm in denial doesn't even detract from its soothing, medicinal relief. Mark and Nikki are fairly impressed. They must have been expecting me to freak out. They're certainly freaking out. But I'm slouched comfortably on the living room couch as they pace in front of me.

"Leo came back," Mark starts in. "Like, twenty minutes after you left."

"He told everybody he synthesized some sort of poison at home," Nikki says.

"See, he got kicked out of graduate school. He was there for chemistry—"

"He got kicked out the week before he was fired—"

"He said it was the same kind of poison that occurs naturally in blowfish—"

"You know, that poison sushi? It's colorless and odorless—"

"He mixed his own homemade stuff into his last batch of fries—"

"It makes you sicker and sicker, and it only takes twenty-four hours—"

"Twenty-four hours! After that, your body just shuts down and you die—"

"There's nothing you can do! Doctors can't even help—"

Jeez. I can't tell which one of them is talking anymore. They've started shouting. Their voices are a jumble, bouncing around between my ringing ears.

Unfortunately, I feel the denial wearing off quicker than I would have liked. Now I'm entering the second stage of grief. And if memory serves correctly . . . Actually I don't remember what the second stage is. Forgetfulness?

Mark and Nikki stop pacing. They draw the same deep, anxious breaths.

"I really think you should come with us, Burger," Mark states. "Just come back to the hospital. Get yourself checked out. Okay?"

"But you just said there's nothing the doctors can do. Right?"

"That's what *Leo* said," Nikki argues, her voice quavering.

I blink at her. I'm at a loss. I ask myself: *Do I really want to go back to St. Vincent's?*

No. No, I don't. Even though I've been poisoned . . . *Poisoned! Holy—*

Forget it. I'm calm. And I have to milk this calmness for all its worth. *Calm, calm, calm.* If I go back to St. Vincent's, I'll definitely lose whatever tenuous grip I have on the calmness. I'll have to deal with that obese security guard again, for starters. No calmness there. Then I'll have to sit in the waiting room. Yikes. Then I'll have to call my parents to secure their permission to get my stomach pumped, or blood transfused, or whatever. And if I can't get in touch with them, my best friend's father will have to sub as my legal guardian, which means he'll have to grant permission to some random surgeon (who I'm sure would much rather be at home in the suburbs having dinner with his wife and kids) to perform whatever desperate "procedures" can be done to save me when there's no chance, no chance at all. . . .

Ugh. Who would want to spend their last hours like that? Not me.

"Burger!" Mark shouts at me. "Come on, dude. This is your life!"

"My life?" I echo blankly. "My life?"

It is my life, isn't it?

That's when it hits me. *My God.*

He's right. Until he said the words, I didn't even look at it that way. I only looked at it in terms of the sniveling coward I am. . . .

Mark is a genius. More than that.

He just triggered an epiphany.

Now I know exactly what needs to be done. *Exactly.* I mean, really; it can't get any more perfect, right? I have a list, don't I?

DANiEL EHRENHAFT

Mark posed the question himself, before he even knew I was poisoned: "Have you ever really *lived*, Burger?" NO! Of course not! It was a sign! A sign from above! Because now I have a chance, an opportunity—a single, glorious, twenty-four-hour period to be brave, like Mark—to make up for my mistakes, my laziness. . . .

Yes, it is MY LIFE. It's truly mine. For the first time ever.

And death will be my catalyst.

I'll bust loose. I'll forget everything. I have to. I owe it to myself. I've followed the same stupid nonroutine every single day, ever since I can remember. Obsessively! Compulsively! Without fail! I hang out at the Circle Eat, I hide in my bedroom with my guitar, I daydream while I play along to Shakes the Clown, I avoid Rachel . . . and so on and so on. It's all evasion, all nothingness. And best of all, I can milk this sudden hysteria; I can use it to quash the panic about what's really happening: that I'm about to head off to that Great Gig in the Sky—

"Ted," Nikki whispers. "You're scaring me. What are you thinking right now?"

"I'm thinking that I don't want to think!" I exclaim, sounding frighteningly like my parents.

Neither she nor Mark says a word.

"Hey, don't be so glum," I add. I leap off the couch. "Buck up, you guys. If what you're saying is true, that I'm gonna die, then what's the point in dwelling on it? I need to start getting busy. Now, bring on the list. I'm serious. Let's finish it, okay? Ay-sap!"

The Second Big Fight of the Last Day of My Life

Before either of them can respond, I dash back to my room for my knapsack.

Whoa. Not a good idea. Leo's synthetic poison makes dashing very difficult. By the time I reach the door, dashing has degenerated into stumbling. I decide to crawl. What the hell? I collapse to the rug and make my way toward the knapsack—I can see the thing, right by my bed—*got it!* Now all I have to do is fumble through the open pocket. . . . *There.* The napkin. I grab it and prop myself up on my elbows, gritting my teeth once more to help fight the dizziness:

<u>BURGER'S SPRING BREAK</u>
1. Lose virginity.
2. Jam with Shakes the Clown.
3. *PARTY* with Shakes the Clown.
4. Get back at Billy Rifkin.

"I have to finish this list," I whisper aloud. "Then I have to do everything on it."

"Ted?" Nikki calls from the living room. "Are you okay?"

"Be right there!" I shout.

I force myself to my feet. I walk—very slowly and cautiously—back down the hall toward the living room. I use the walls as a crutch. And in the process, something else extraordinary happens. Somehow I manage to see those walls for the first time. I really, truly *observe* the walls of the Burger family apartment. Framed photos are everywhere, like a plague: dozens of them, hundreds, maybe even thousands. It's just . . .

I've never noticed them before. Not like this. I mean, how often do you really take a good, objective look at your own home? How often do you step back and soak in the place you've lived your entire life? But death has given me a new perspective. If I felt my life flashing before my eyes back at the diner, when Leo pulled the water gun, well, now it's happening outside my mind and in real time. My life is *literally flashing before my eyes.* Frame by frame.

And not just my own. The lives of every person my parents have ever met: every friend, every client, every casual acquaintance—even Mr. Hammurabi, the deli guy across the street—they're all included, too, somewhere.

I pause in front of a part of wall space dedicated entirely to me.

So many pictures . . .

There I am, holding my electric guitar right after Mom and

Dad unveiled it for my eleventh birthday. There I am, strumming it happily. There I am, sticking my tongue out at Mom as she yells at me to stop playing so I can watch an important commercial.

And sure enough, there I am again, one picture away, in front of the TV.

There are even several shots of Rachel and me. She's wearing the same infinitely nice smile in all of them. My eyes grow misty. Now I finally understand *why* my mom and dad mount so many photos on the wall. Each represents a perfect, illustrative moment. The display is like a trailer for the movie of their lives. And now my own personal trailer is about to be yanked from theaters—

"Ted!" Nikki shouts.

She's standing right in front of me. I nearly fall over. She loops my arm around her shoulders and escorts me back to the sofa, the way a medic might escort a wounded soldier away from battle.

Mark has started pacing again.

"You gotta call your parents, dude," he says, stroking his chin, distracted. "You gotta let them know what happened. This is bad. I mean, this is really bad, you know?"

I nod. "Yeah, I know it's bad."

"So?"

"So what's the point of calling them? I mean, seriously.

They're never around when I need them. They're never even around when I *don't* need them. They're just never around. Even when they *are* here, they aren't really here. You know? They're so wrapped up in each other and their work that they don't see anything other than themselves, or their agenda, or their pictures on the wall . . . and if you want to know the truth, you guys are more of a family to me than they are. I'm not kidding. I spend more time with you. I learn more from you. I—"

I shut up.

Mark and Nikki are both staring at me. Their lips are trembling.

What the hell did I just say? Now I know for sure the poison is taking effect because something is wrong with my brain— something other than what's usually wrong with it. I'm never this open or honest or analytical. *Whatever.* I can't afford to think too hard about that kind of BS right now. The clock is ticking.

"I mean, why do you think I ran to get *this*?" I continue, just to fill the silence. I wave the napkin in front of them. "I have to make the most of what little time I have left! I have to live it up!"

"I know you do, Burger!" Mark yells at me. "That's why you need to get off your ass and come with us and stop being such a moron!"

I scowl and lean back in the sofa, exhausted for some reason.

The vertigo isn't so bad now. Neither is the tinnitus. Maybe anger mutes the poison. But I'm angry because I realize that I shouldn't be angry at all. Mark and I aren't arguing; we're *agreeing*. He's right. We both are. I need to get off my ass and stop being a moron.

"Mark, I'm sorry," I apologize forcefully. "But we're gonna finish this list. You told me I had to. Remember? You even told me I should live the next twenty-four hours like they were my last because my parents are away. Well, now they *are* my last."

"Burger, that was a joke," he breathes.

"I know. And that's the whole point. It's time to make this joke as funny and as cool and awesome and *meaningful* as we possibly can. So let's figure out ten things for me to do, and then let me start doing them."

Down to Business

Mark responds by kneeling in front of my parents' liquor cabinet.

"What are you doing?" I ask.

"I'm going to get drunk," he states very matter-of-factly. "If you aren't going to the hospital, then you leave me no choice. And you're gonna get drunk, too."

"I am?"

"Yeah. We all are. It'll help us think." He leans forward and

DANIEL EHRENHAFT

peers closely at the mahogany door. It's got an old-fashioned brass lock. For a moment he hesitates. Then he makes a fist and punches the lock, knuckles first: *Smack!* The door gently swings open, without so much as a creak.

Mark turns and beams at me.

I have to smile back. Mark may be an impulsive maniac, but he's got flair.

"Now, let's see . . ."

He reaches in and grabs a bottle of foul-looking liquid. It's roughly the same color as gasoline. Judging from the classy font on its label, though, it must be expensive. I lean forward and squint at the lettering. *Glenmorangie?* Never heard of it. Mark stands up straight. He waves the stuff in front of all of us, swishing it around like a magician about to perform a signature trick. Then, in a single deft maneuver, he yanks out the cork cap—*thwok!*—and shoves the bottle against his lips, tilting it up and chugging furiously. *Glug glug glug* . . . he sputters. His face shrivels like a popped balloon. Brown liquid drips to the floor. He looks as if he's just been forced to ingest sewer sludge. Yet somehow he musters a demented grin.

"Yeah!" he chokes out. "This stuff rocks!"

I glance at Nikki. She shrugs.

"I've had scotch before," she says nonchalantly. "It's better with ice."

Mark thrusts it into my hands. "It's fine without ice, though," he croaks, his voice hoarse. "Just take a pull, Burger. Right now."

"I . . ." I turn to Nikki again. Her saucer eyes are moist. She looks as if she's about to cry. I can tell that this is a decision I'll have to make on my own. (I hate that kind of decision.) My gaze falls to the heavy bottle. I catch a whiff of what's inside. *Jesus*—my parents actually *pay* for this crap?

"Come on, Burger," Mark whispers. He claps me on the shoulder. "Get down to business. Do this. It'll help me out. I mean it."

I can't argue. Clearly Mark does need help. Why is his reaction to this whole poisoning thing so much more out of control than mine? But I suppose I shouldn't think too hard about that. Screw it. I should just take a pull. It's not as if it'll endanger my health. I don't *have* any health anymore.

I upend the bottle, trying to imitate what I just saw him do. Shockingly, I don't barf. Scotch seems to be one of those rare liquids that taste better than they smell. Sure, it burns a little going down, but then it feels warm in my belly. And the warmth lingers. More shocking still, it buries the nausea. After two more swigs I find that it actually helps me, too. There's still a little vertigo, a little tinnitus—but as long as I stay seated . . . this is the best I've felt since I've been poisoned.

"Now you're talking!" Mark exclaims. He swipes the bottle back. "I'll grab us some glasses, okay, Burger? Nice ones. Highball glasses. And some ice, too."

He scurries into the kitchen.

DANIEL EHRENHAFT

Meanwhile Nikki stares at me, blinking the wetness away.

I have no idea what she's thinking. I have no idea what any of us is thinking. It's a unique experience. Usually I can at least speak for myself.

Moments later Mark returns with glasses and ice. We squeeze into the couch together: boy-girl-boy. He pours us all generous servings.

The ice crackles as we lift our scotches for a toast.

"To life!" he shouts.

I have to smile. *I've* never even had such lousy comic timing.

Nikki shakes her head, embarrassed for all of us.

"What?" Mark says. He sounds genuinely puzzled.

"The toast, you dope." Nikki groans.

He blinks. "Oh. Well, what should I have said? To death?" He slurps his drink, draining about half of it. "Hand over that napkin. We're here for Burger, remember? And if he isn't gonna think about dying, then neither am I."

Heroism, Nigeria, Bank Robbing, and Suicide

Within the half hour, we've each downed two jumbo-sized scotches apiece. Mark has been a dervish of energy: putting on CDs, taking them off, refilling our drinks . . . and now he's back on the couch, scribbling on the napkin. As the level of liquor in the bottle falls, the volume in the room rises. Soon we're all shouting at one another. We can't stop giggling, either. The three of us seem to be experiencing the same simultaneous hearing loss. *Hey!* I think, a lopsided grin on my face. *Hearing loss is another one of the symptoms of Ménière's disease!* So now I'm three for four. And what was the last one? Pressure in the ears?

"Mark!" Nikki yells. "What are you writing?"

She's slouched deep into the couch now. She's slouched so deep that she's practically horizontal. Her tank top is rumpled. Her scotch rests on her exposed navel. She taps the glass with her silver rings, smiling up at him.

Mark tilts the napkin so all three of us can read what he's jotting down:

5. Do something truly heroic. Like rescue a baby from a burning building.
6. Along these lines, actually *GO* to one of those third world countries Rachel is always talking about and do something positive *THERE*. (Like Nigeria or wherever. But fast.)
7. Rob a bank.

Somehow I muster the strength to speak. "Whoa, whoa, hold on. Rob a bank? Why do I have to do that?"

He looks at me as if I've lost my mind. "You have to do something *bad* to counterbalance the *good*, Burger," he replies, slurring slightly. "Part of living life to the fullest is embracing the Dark Side."

I momentarily forget the poison. "The Dark Side? What is this, *Star Wars*?"

Mark turns to Nikki, raising his hands as if to say: A little help?

"Ted, you have to do something totally beyond the confines of morality," Nikki explains, as if she and Mark have plotted this robbery numerous times in the past. "But listen. You aren't gonna be alone. We're gonna be with you all the way, one hundred percent. When it comes time to knock over the bank, *we're* gonna knock it over with you. I mean, aside from the obvious—you know, that a strong-through-the-door operation always requires a lookout, a driver, and a vault man—aside from all *that*, which we'll worry about later . . ."

I blink at her.

Knock over? Strong-through-the-door operation? Vault man?

She's even drunker than I am.

Nikki grabs the napkin and snatches the pen away from Mark and starts scribbling something herself.

8. Pull a crazy stunt, like bungee jump off the GW Bridge.

"See, Ted, your problem is that you don't like putting your-self in dangerous situations," she informs me. "You have to laugh publicly in the face of death—like that magician, David What's-his-face. You know? The guy who froze himself in a block of ice? That's the key to living a full life. Damn, what's his name? David . . ."

"David Blaine?" I say.

She nods. "Yeah, him."

"That's the key to living a full life?"

She nods again.

"Freezing yourself in a block of ice," I repeat. "Bungee jumping off the George Washington Bridge."

"Exactly," Nikki says. "You know. Something stupid, like what Mark would do."

We both giggle again, like idiots.

I spot Mark in the corner, talking on the phone. When did he start making calls? He gives me a thumbs-up. There's a satis-fied "we're all set!" gleam in his eye. Clearly he's just confirmed something of extreme importance, but I have no idea what it could be or who he's talking to. He mutters something incom-prehensible and hangs up.

"Dude!" he yells, elated.

"What's going on?"

"I just found out where Billy Rifkin lives," he says.

"Billy Rifkin?" I don't know why, but this makes me laugh

DANiEL EHRENHAFT

harder than I've laughed all night. I double over in hysterics. Scotch spills onto the floor.

"Get outta here!" Nikki yells.

"You know what that means, don't you?" Mark asks me.

Nikki swats me on the shoulder. "It means Ted's gotta go get him!"

I stop laughing. "Huh?"

"That's right, dude," Mark concurs. His eyes are unsteady. "This is what you've been waiting for. 525 West Seventy-third Street. Number 15E. You've gotta get back at that little pecker for making you look like a fool. I mean, you remember how you felt that day, right? With everybody laughing at you? With your guitar strings in the sewer—"

"Yeah, yeah, I remember."

I try to straighten up on the couch. A sudden onslaught of vertigo sends me crashing into Nikki. Oops. Best just to get off the couch altogether. With a mighty grunt I propel myself up to a standing position. (Or close enough. The teetering makes full uprightness impossible.) "What about the other stuff on that napkin?" I ask, trying not to slur my words. "What about partying with Shakes the Clown? Billy is number four, right? Shouldn't I party with Shakes the Clown first?"

Mark raises his eyebrows. "Uh . . . Ted?" He shoves the napkin back in his pocket and waves a drunken hand around the room. "I don't see Shakes the Clown here. If you're hiding them somewhere, fine. Let's get started. Otherwise we have to be realistic. We have to work with what we've got. Know what I'm saying?"

I do my best to stick my tongue out at him. It's difficult. I'm smiling uncontrollably.

"Now, listen, Burger," Mark says. "Don't worry about a thing." He lurches forward and throws a sweaty arm around my shoulders. "We're gonna take care of that other stuff, too. Even the first thing! That's right. You're going to become a man tonight. But you gotta trust me on this. Okay? Will you trust me? Will you trust your old pal Mark? You gotta beat the crap outta this kid. Say the address back to me: 525 West Seventy-third Street. Apartment 15E. And—Burger!"

"What?"

"Have you heard a word I've said?"

"Have I heard . . . ?" I crack up again. "That's funny. Rachel asked me that exact same thing earlier."

Mark opens his mouth. Then he closes it and blinks a few times, gulping loudly. "Listen up," he says, his voice strained. "We have a plan now. *You're* gonna go uptown and beat the crap out of Billy Rifkin. In the meantime *we're* gonna stay here and deal with the rest of this list for you. We're even gonna figure out nine and ten. We're gonna finish this thing. I swear it. Okay?"

I lift my shoulders, in no position to argue. In spite of the fact that Mark seems to be on the verge of a breakdown, I'm still laughing.

DANIEL EHRENHAFT

Call Me a Nut

Call me a nut, but I love the New York City transit system. Most people see it as a hassle. Some people even refuse to take the subway. But they don't know what they're missing. A subway car is the prime spot for such excellent pastimes as:

1. People watching
2. Bonding with perfect strangers when something goes wrong. And something *always* goes wrong. That's the beauty of it. You're sitting next to a grizzled businessman—the kind of guy you have nothing in common with—when the train suddenly breaks down. You and the businessman exchange a smile. You roll your eyes. And just like that, you're war buddies, comrades in arms, united by the heroic struggle to get from point A to point B.
3. Eavesdropping on bizarre conversations. And you always hear one.

So when I board the uptown Seventh Avenue local, heading in the general direction of Billy Rifkin's apartment, I know I'm in for a treat. As a matter of fact, I don't even plan to get off. I'm just going to ride for a while, and people watch, and bond, and eavesdrop (for the last time ever in my life!) . . . and somewhere in there, I'm going to make up the brilliant and hilarious tale of how I beat the crap out of Billy Rifkin—and when I get back home, Mark and Nikki are going to love me for it.

The Land of Extraordinary Coincidence

I first notice the couple at Fourteenth Street.

Did they get on before? I'm not sure. (Remember: I'm drunk.) They're older than me, and judging from their too-cool and self-righteous vibe, I figure they're students at Columbia or NYU. You can spot these college types a mile away. They never sit down on the subway. They insist on standing because it tells the world that they're considerate enough to leave seats open for the elderly or disabled, even when the car is nearly empty, as it is now. *Fakers.* The girl, a hair-dyed-black goth, is heavily tattooed. The guy is small and pale, all glasses and dirty blond bangs. I catch a snippet of dialogue:

". . . I'm not being a martyr," the girl is saying.

"Yeah, you are," the guy snaps back. He glances around to make sure nobody is eavesdropping. I stare at my lap. "You're laying a guilt trip on me. I mean, come on, Charlotte. You know I have my hands full with Amnesty International."

Amnesty International?

Naturally, my ears perk up.

Now, this might strike you as an extraordinary coincidence, the fact that two young people—a couple, no less—are fighting about something near and dear to my own girlfriend's heart. And it is. But that's the beauty of the transit system. Really, it's the beauty of New York City as a whole. It's the Land of Extraordinary Coincidence.

DANiEL EHRENHAFT

"Oh, I get it," the girl says, sulking. "You can't help me out because you've used up all your altruism. You volunteer for an organization that just serves as a celebrity platform for . . . for . . . for *narcissism*. Amnesty International doesn't accomplish anything, Thumb. It's a bogus organization."

Wait.

Did she just call him *Thumb*? Spelled like *Thom*, maybe?

Perhaps it's the poison acting up . . . but no, I'm pretty sure she did. *Thom. Thom Thumb. That'th thilly.* I bite my cheek.

"How would you know?" the guy says through his teeth. "And if you want to talk narcissism, why don't you take a good long look in the mirror? Oh, but that's right! You already do! You spend an hour in the mirror every morning! You're the biggest narcissist I know!"

"But I have to sit at the mirror every morning. It's the only way I can focus my *qi*." (Pronounced "chee.") "You *know* that, Thom."

"Charlotte—"

"LADIES AND GENTLEMEN." An automated voice booms from above. "DUE TO TRACK SIGNAL PROBLEMS, THE NEXT STOP ON THIS TRAIN WILL BE FORTY-SECOND STREET. THIS TRAIN WILL NO LONGER BE RUNNING ON THE LOCAL TRACK. IF YOU WISH TO GET OFF AT INTERMEDIARY STATIONS, PLEASE CROSS THE PLATFORM AT TIMES SQUARE AND TAKE THE LOCAL DOWNTOWN TRAIN. THIS TRAIN WILL BE RUNNING EXPRESS."

A collective groan rises from the passengers.

What did I tell you? Something always goes wrong.

Now it's bonding time. I catch Thom's eyes. I search them for a flicker of recognition, an acknowledgment of shared suffering. We're war buddies, after all. *I feel for you, my man,* I tell him with my sympathetic gaze. *We're in this together.*

"What are you looking at, asshole?" he asks.

My Obligation

Until now, I haven't fully taken stock of what's happening to me. Yes, I've known and accepted that I've been poisoned. . . .

Or have I really? No, I don't think I have. I'm still floundering in denial. But Thom's question has brought my fate into stark relief. Not just for the obvious reason: that no matter how much I romanticize this last subway ride, I've just been called an asshole. It's not even so much that my intestines suddenly feel as if they've been tied into neat little bows. It's because I feel like saying something back.

Normally if I were asked "what [I was] looking at" by a pretentious jerk, I'd probably just stare at my sneakers. At worst, I might mutter "not much" under my breath—inaudibly, of course. But at this moment, I don't harbor any ill will. Clearly this is a guy who feels too much stress and anger. You can see it in the tight lines on his face, in the flatness of his bespectacled eyes. *Thom, life is too short for all that,* I think. I know how short it is, firsthand. I've got maybe twenty-one hours left. I've been granted a great gift of wisdom. And it's my obligation—better yet, my duty—to share it.

Thom raises his eyebrows. They vanish under his bangs. "You got a problem?"

"No, I don't," I say. "I'm at peace."

He laughs shortly. "Excuse me?"

"Everybody, listen up!" I hear myself yell.

Poisoned blood pounds in my head. I stand in the middle of the car. I've never done anything like this in my life. I've never intentionally made a spectacle of myself. I've been made a spectacle *of*, many times—but it's finally time for me to wipe the symbolic pie off my clown face. It's time to talk back, to take action.

Unfortunately, the only two people who seem to be paying attention are Charlotte and Thom. Everybody else looks away. Why wouldn't they? A disheveled teenager has embarked on a loud monologue for no apparent reason.

"Listen up!" I repeat, fighting to milk the alcohol and adrenaline for all their energy. "I don't want any money, and I'm not trying to sell anything! I just want to say that there's no point in fighting! If you're involved with somebody, I mean! Because, you know, if you're in a relationship, even if you don't necessarily love that other person with all your heart . . . you have to be considerate! You have to respect that person! You have to respect peace! And maybe you have to let them go! But if you do—"

"THIS IS FORTY-SECOND STREET, TIMES SQUARE," the automated voice announces.

I frown at the loudspeakers. The train screeches to a halt.

The force of the braking sends me toppling to the floor.

My knees hit first. My palms scrape on the grimy linoleum.

"Ouch," I grunt.

Miracle of miracles, the fall stops there. I'm able to maintain balance on all fours, like a child, awaiting a well-deserved spanking. To be honest, I half expect somebody in the car to take advantage of this precarious position. Fortunately, nobody does. Every single passenger scurries out the door.

"Charlotte, promise me we'll take a cab next time, okay?" I hear Thom mutter. "There are too many freaks on the subway."

Surprise Attack

Screw it. I've changed my mind. I *am* going to beat the crap out of Billy Rifkin. Why the hell not, right? I'll be dead by this time tomorrow. One concern: hopefully he hasn't had a growth spurt in the last five years. He was five inches shorter than me

DANIEL EHRENHAFT

the last time I saw him. Whatever. Even if he is bigger, I've got certain strategic advantages. He isn't expecting me. A surprise attack is always best—as I learned from Mark today at the diner, when he wrestled Leo to the ground. Plus I'm fueled with rage. My judgment, or what's left of it, is definitely impaired.

And I know what you're thinking, but you're wrong; I'm *not* enraged because I'm lying on a subway-car floor after some little wiener with a loser girlfriend called me names—when I only tried to help them. (Well, okay, maybe I'm enraged a little about that.) Mostly I'm enraged about *everything*. And I'm enraged at *everyone*: at myself, because I was such a jerk to my girlfriend earlier this afternoon; at my parents, with their jabbering on and on about billboards; at Leo, because he poisoned me. . . .

Ugh.

Mark was right that day he dared me to approach Rachel. There *is* a swirling vortex inside my head. And now there's poison. And this freaking tinnitus. And several glasses of scotch. It's getting pretty crowded in there.

I push myself up and collapse back into a cold plastic seat.

Next stop, Seventy-second Street. Billy Rifkin lives on Seventy-third. Number 525. Apartment 15E. Yes, I remembered the address, even at less than full capacity. I'll be there in no time.

As the train pulls out of the station, I spot Thom on the

platform. I give him the finger. He reciprocates. So completes the bonding of two comrades-in-arms.

The "Seal-a-Deal" Strategy

Just my crappy luck: 525 West Seventy-third is one of those luxury skyscrapers with a doorman. My heart sinks as I trudge up to the entrance. The place must be sixty stories tall—a massive steel-and-glass tower whose apartments glow high above me, secure and impenetrable. Now I'll have to convince a doorman to convince the Rifkins to let me up. *Stupid.* I should have planned for this earlier. I pause outside the floor-to-ceiling lobby windows, racking my brain for a legitimate-sounding lie. Can I say that I'm an old friend? Nah, the Rifkins probably wouldn't even recognize my name. Can I pretend to be a delivery boy? No, that would only work if the Rifkins had ordered food. . . .

Suddenly I realize that the doorman is staring right at me.

He's rotund, uniformed in a red suit (complete with tassels and a cap), and sports a Santa Claus beard. Except that he isn't nearly as jolly as old Saint Nick. In another few seconds he'll probably call the cops to inform them that a suspicious-looking juvenile is loitering near the premises.

Well. This is it.

Either I grab life by the proverbial *cajones,* as Mark said, or I slink away in shame. And I can just picture what will happen if I do the latter. Yup: I'll get back on the subway, and I won't say a word to anyone. I won't eavesdrop, and I won't cause problems—and instead I'll daydream about all the things I should be doing, and when I finally get home, I'll find Mark and Nikki buck naked in my parents' bedroom. . . .

Billy Rifkin, here I come.

I breeze through the revolving doors, conjuring the perfect lie from thin air, like magic. *Thank God for booze, rage, and poison!* The lobby is richly furnished and ice cold. It smells like carpet cleaner, the way all luxury high-rise lobbies do. I stroll up to the front desk.

"Can I help you?" Sour Santa asks.

"Yes, thank you. My name is Mark Singer. I'm raising money for Amnesty International. Are you familiar with our organization?"

"I'm sorry," he says. "We don't allow solicitors here."

I chuckle apologetically. "No, of course not. I understand. But I'm not here to solicit money from random strangers. I'm here to see the Rifkins? Number 15E? I went to grade school with their son Billy, and part of my assignment is to raise awareness about our organization among kids my age."

The guy doesn't answer. His face might as well be carved from Sheetrock. I wonder if he'll ask me for ID. I actually have my passport on me. I always carry it in my back pocket (probably not the wisest idea) because I don't have a driver's license yet. The problem is that it's *my* passport, not Mark's.

"If you would just buzz them, I'd really appreciate it," I continue, not missing a beat. My tone is courteous, nonconfrontational. "And if they aren't home or if they have no interest in talking to me, I'll just be on my way. I won't take up a minute more of your time. Thanks so much!"

Finally he picks up the intercom phone.

I congratulate myself. I hate to admit it, but Mom and Dad deserve credit for that smooth performance. Because if there's one thing I've learned from having parents in the advertising industry, it's that it's always better to thank people preemptively if you're trying to weasel something out of them. They even have a name for it. They call it the "seal-a-deal" strategy. The theory: thanking people *before* a deal has been sealed creates the impression that the deal already *has* been sealed. So then people feel guilty refusing you. They feel obligated to accommodate you. Clever, huh? Yes, every child of advertisers is also part amateur psychologist. It comes with the territory.

"Hello, Mrs. Rifkin? It's Freddy from the front desk. I have somebody here to see Billy . . ." He cups his hand over the phone and raises his eyebrows at me.

"Mark Singer," I whisper. "From Amnesty International. And PS 109."

"Mark Singer," he repeats into the mouthpiece. "From Amnesty International? And PS 109?"

I hold my breath, my smile intact.

"Okay, then, Mrs. Rifkin. I'll send him right up." He hangs up the phone and finally cracks a smile. "The elevators are around the corner to the right, Mark."

Sweet, Sweet, Sweet!

It isn't until I'm shooting toward the fifteenth floor that I consider what I'm doing. I'm on my way to see Billy Rifkin, ostensibly to kick his ass. No, not ostensibly—I *will* kick his ass. Because as the plush elevator picks up speed and blood drains from my enfeebled brain, I'm overcome with suppressed memories . . . not just the guitar-strings-in-the-sewer incident, but a host of others: the time Billy hurled a stink bomb into a bathroom stall I was using, the time he spray painted the words *Super Butt* on the principal's office wall and somehow managed to implicate me, the time he slapped me on the back of the legs with his skateboard, bruising—

Ding!

The doors slide open.

I step into the carpeted hall.

My heart starts to pound. I take a moment to scope the

area for an escape route. I hone in on a lighted exit sign next to apartment 15E: the fire stairs. Perfect. I'll ring the doorbell. If Billy answers, I'll punch him in the face—*hard*—and be on my way. If his mom answers, I'll ask to speak to him. Then she'll summon him to the front door, at which point I'll punch him in the face—*hard*—et cetera.

So what if he's grown a foot since the sixth grade? I've got the element of surprise on my side. Just like Mark did when he attacked Leo.

And after I've knocked him cold, I'll race down the fifteen flights of stairs (not too far), and I'll sneak out through the back door or parking garage (not a problem), and in less than twenty seconds I'll be back on the subway, heading home. Ha! They'll never catch me. It's not like Sour Santa in the lobby could chase me down. No way. He's too fat. I'll be a Phantom, a regular Angel of Punching in the Face. *Oh, man. This is gonna be sweet! Sweet, sweet, sweet!*

Good thing I'm still plastered. I take a deep breath and tip-toe to the apartment door. I clench my right hand into a fist. I ring the bell with my left.

The door opens . . .

And I get exactly what I wish for.

It's Billy Rifkin himself. Right in front of me. In the flesh. Five years after his egregious crimes. Only if he's had a growth spurt, I can't tell, because he's sitting in a wheelchair.

Not to Sound Like Jesus or Anything

"Ted?" he says.

The first thing I notice about him (aside from the obvious) is that he now wears glasses. Circular, wire-rimmed, John Lennon–style glasses. Behind them, his green eyes are serene. I don't remember serenity in his eyes before. I remember hate and cruelty. He's smiling, too. It's not the spiteful smile of the little twerp I knew back in grade school, either. No, this smile is warm and inviting. Aside from that, though, I guess he looks pretty much the same. Small and skinny. Well, except that his hair is shoulder length. He's also wearing a tie-dyed T-shirt that features a charcoal portrait of Martin Luther King.

Martin Luther King.

This is not Billy Rifkin. This is a kind, peace-loving hippie. An innocent kid to whom something terrible has happened. This is the boy I just tried to be on the subway. This is the boy I lamely and miserably failed to be.

Billy laughs. "You are Ted Burger, right? Ted Burger from PS 109?"

"Yeah." The vertigo, tinnitus, and nausea return full force. I swallow, clutching the door frame to maintain balance.

"Your friend Mark is here, too, right?" He peers around me into the hall. "The doorman said Mark Singer was here. I remember you guys were tight. It's so cool that you still hang out. And that you work for Amnesty International, too!"

"Yeah—ah, well, Mark's down in the car," I lie to him. "Mark had to stay with the car. See, we drove, and . . . you know, it's so hard to find parking around here—so, um, he's illegally parked. That's where Mark is . . . in the car. Waiting."

"Yeah, sorry," Billy apologizes, as if it's perfectly natural to have a stammering moron show up out of your past. "Parking around here can be a real drag. Man, I wish I knew you guys were coming! I could have reserved a spot for you down in the garage! I mean, I'm sure you don't have a lot of time to hang out." He laughs again—that horrible, friendly laugh. My stomach twists in another painful knot. "I know what's like to canvass. I used to canvass for Greenpeace, out in Jersey. You have to hit as many residences as possible to make your quota. Right?"

I nod, even though I have no clue what he's talking about. I'm flabbergasted. He's in a wheelchair. He's paralyzed. He's become a saint.

His brow furrows. "Hey, are you okay? You don't look so hot."

"I . . . uh . . . I . . ."

"Aw, don't sweat the chair, bro," Billy says comfortingly.

Now I'm fairly certain I'll throw up. He's trying to make this easy on me. *He's* trying to make *me* feel better—about *his* disability. This can't be happening. Maybe I've already died. Maybe I'm in hell right now, being tortured for a lifetime of wickedness.

"It was a skateboard accident a couple of years ago," he adds with a rueful grin. "Long story. But in a weird way, it was one of the best things that happened to me." He sighs. His eyes twinkle. "I mean, not totally, of course."

Please shut up. Please just slam the door in my face and tell me to get lost—

"It is true, though, in a way," he continues. "See, when you lose the ability to walk, and to skate, and to run, and whatever—and most of all, when you lose the ability to be a little prick making everyone else's life miserable . . ." He chuckles. "Well, you get some perspective on life. I mean, I think back on the way I was before the accident, and it makes me sick. You know? And I never realized it until I was lying there in the hospital, with all the time in the world on my hands. It's like . . . not to sound like Jesus or anything, but it was almost like I died and was resurrected. Or not so much resurrected as reborn. You know? Does that make any sense?"

No! I don't know! How could I possibly know that? Just let me go! That's all I ask! Please! I'm sorry! I should have never come here! I'm drunk and poisoned—

"I'm rambling, I know," Billy says, rolling his eyes. "I'm sorry to waste your time, bro. I'm just psyched to see an old face. And I'm totally down for contributing to Amnesty International. That organization *rocks.* They get real, legitimate celebrities behind them, which totally raises awareness . . . ooh, boy." He shakes his head. "As if you don't know that already! There I go again! Rambling and preaching to the converted!" He spins around and cups his hands around his mouth. "Mom!" he yells. "Bust out the checkbook, okay? These guys are in a rush! They're old friends, and one of them is illegally parked downstairs!"

A foul taste rises in my throat. I clamp my hand over my mouth.

Billy turns and winks at me. "Once my mom hears 'illegally parked,' she gets all stressed," he whispers. "She's gotten, like, forty tickets outside our building. I bet we can get her to write you a check for a hundred bucks. She'll do anything just to make sure you get back to your car fast."

Nutshell

No, I don't barf. And in case you were wondering how low I could possibly sink, I don't punch Billy Rifkin in the face, either.

In a nutshell:

Mrs. Rifkin approaches the door with her checkbook. She, too, is a hippie. She's got a beautiful long mane of gray-black hair. She's wearing a purple batik skirt and a homemade sweater—and her smile is one of those full-face smiles. It's utterly genuine. She shakes my hand with a sincerity that my

DANiEL EHRENHAFT

parents can't even begin to approach. Then she expounds upon the Rifkin family commitment to Amnesty International. She emphasizes the celebrity factor. "If Tim Robbins and Gabriel Byrne appear on TV as members, then the public will learn about crimes against humanity. I think it's great!"

Mrs. Rifkin quickly writes a check out for two hundred dollars so as to expedite my return to the nonexistent illegally parked car.

I thank them, shake both their hands, and promise Billy I'll keep in touch.

Billy apologizes one final time for being so talkative.

I hurry to the elevator.

When the doors close, I realize that my cheeks are wet and that my throat is clogged. I don't stop sniffling until I'm back on the subway, heading downtown.

The Meaning of Joy

When I finally arrive home a half hour later, I find Mark in my living room, dancing with a strange Asian woman.

It's a little past eight o'clock. The stereo is cranked. It's some rap song I've never heard before. There isn't much to it: just the same three-note bass hook a hundred times in a row. Every time it hits the lowest of the three notes, the photos on the walls rattle in their frames. The chorus exhorts "da peeps" to "get buck wild."

Neither Mark nor the woman hears me come in. They're dancing on opposite sides of the coffee table—eyes closed, butts wiggling, lost in their own trances. The bottle of Glenmorangie sits between them, empty. I wonder where Nikki is. I try not to stare at the Asian woman. It's difficult. For starters, there's her outfit: an obscenely tight white T-shirt, cut high above her midriff, complemented by stilettos and a leather miniskirt. Her face is mesmerizing, too, coated in so much makeup that it looks as if she's wearing a mask. How old is she? Twenty? Thirty? Sixty? It's impossible to tell. At least she and Mark aren't touching each other, which for some reason makes me feel very relieved.

Well. I'm sure I'll get an explanation about all this sooner or later. Right now I have to get on with the list. Time is slipping away, and I haven't made a whole lot of progress. I can feel the poison working through me, pulsing through my veins, sapping my strength. Why couldn't Leo have synthesized a poison that kills a person instantly? It's not fair. *Nothing* is fair. Nothing is really going according to plan, either. But I suppose it's good that at least some people are enjoying themselves. I tiptoe past the dancers, down the hall toward my bedroom—

Nikki rounds the corner. She nearly slams into me. She's pulling on her jean jacket, as if she's about to leave. "Ted! Thank God you're back. You didn't have your cell phone on you! I was just about to go look for you, actually. We've got to get you out of here. Mark is . . . I don't know. But I'm not too happy with him right now."

"Why? What's going on? I don't understand. I just walked in the door two seconds ago. Mark didn't even hear me come in. Who's that woman?"

"She's a prostitute, Ted. A *hooker*."

"Oh," I say.

Is it my imagination, or is Nikki mad at me? Why? *I* have no idea why Mark is dancing with a hooker in my living room. Still, I can't help feeling responsible. It is my home, after all. Maybe it's just some lingering guilt over what went on at Billy Rifkin's. I'm definitely guilty of something—I just don't know what it is. I'm used to feeling this way, though. I even have a name for it: guilt by self-association.

"Mark ordered her online for you with his dad's credit card," Nikki says. She drags me into my bedroom and points at the computer screen, then slams the door behind both of us— muffling the bass line but not by that much. "See?"

SHOWGIRL ESCORTS!!!™

I nod, chewing my lip. I'm not sure whether to laugh or go kill him.

He ordered a hooker online for me. With his dad's money.

Beneath the logo there's an accompanying photo, except

that the woman's face is blanked out. I can only see scantily clad body parts. But it includes a brief description, in language worthy of my parents:

JOY: 5'4"/36-24-36/105 lbs
This Asian beauty will leave you breathless with her sultry dancing and mystical philosophy! She knows the meaning of discreet! $400.00/hr.

The door flies open.

"Dude!" Mark yells, bounding into the room. He's dripping with sweat. The hooker slinks in behind him. "When did you get back? I didn't even hear you come in!"

I shrug, unable to talk.

"So this is your boy, huh?" the hooker asks Mark. Her voice is deep, husky.

"That's him, Joy," Mark says. He grins at her. "What do you think?"

Joy looks me up and down with the same butcherlike neutrality that the intern at St. Vincent's did. Then she smiles.

"I like what I see," she breathes. She steps toward me.

I step back.

"What are you scared of, sugar?" she whispers. "I'm gonna teach you the Meaning of Joy tonight. You dig?"

"I . . ." I gaze at her in horror, feeling like a trapped animal.

Suddenly, somehow, I've found myself in the impossible position of having to talk my way *out* of sex. Me! A sixteen-year-old boy! A virgin! The human race's most sex-obsessed demographic! But if that's what I have to do, then so be it. I'll talk myself silly. Because there is no way I am getting near this woman. NONE.

"What's the problem, Burger?" Mark asks. "Don't you wanna get laid?"

"Of course I want to get laid! That's not the point!" I take a deep breath, struggling to calm myself. "I'm just . . . Listen, I appreciate what you're trying to do here. Really. And I'm sorry if—you know—money has changed hands or whatever. But I'm not gonna do this. That's all there is to it."

Mark looks baffled. "Why not?"

I frown at him. I don't even know where to start. Gee, Mark: because hiring a complete stranger to have sex with is wrong, maybe? Because the whole idea behind businesses like Showgirl Escorts!!!™ is utterly sordid—evil and exploitative for a thousand different reasons? Because the first time you have sex, it should be with somebody you love, with somebody you trust (or at the very least, with somebody you *know*), and it should be a Pure act . . . yes, Pure with a capital *P,* because sex is the Pure act, the ultimate expression of intimacy and—

"Because maybe Ted doesn't want to lose his virginity to a hooker!" Nikki yells.

Dr. Groove Meister, PhD

That sums it up.

Joy laughs. "Damn! You go, girl!"

"Nikki, why is this any of your business?" Mark says.

"It's not," Nikki snaps back. "But it's *Ted's*, right? Shouldn't you have asked him if he wanted you to do this? It's his virginity to lose, isn't it? It's his body, right?"

Blood surges to my face for what seems like the thousandth time today. I cling to the desk. I cling the way a drowning man would cling to a life preserver. It's not even so much the embarrassment that's killing me right now (I'm plenty used to that); it's that I've never seen the two of them fight like this. Even when they bicker, there's a lot of horsing around. But this is ugly and uncomfortable—and it's the last thing I want to deal with, given that I'm about to drop dead. I wish *they* had been on the subway to hear my speech about love and respect. I've based my entire existence on the premise that Mark and Nikki are too mature to fight like this. I aspire toward what they have. They're my *ideal*.

"Yes, it is his body, Nikki," Mark grumbles. "That's the whole point."

Joy marches back out into the hall. "Hey, I'm down for whatever. But at the hour of nine, it's pumpkin time. If y'all are still looking for fun, y'all are welcome to . . ." Her voice is lost in the hip-hop still blaring from the living room.

DANIEL EHRENHAFT

Welcome to what?

I feel sicker than I have since this whole poison business started. Is she talking about some of that "mystical philosophy" she's so famous for, as advertised on the Showgirl Escorts!!!™ web site? Ha! Ha . . . *Oh, man.* I shouldn't joke about this, even to myself. There's nothing funny about the situation.

"Ted, do you want to see Shakes the Clown?" Nikki asks me. "Because that's where I'm going to take you, right now."

"You are?"

"Yeah. They start in less than an hour."

"They do?"

"They're playing at the Onyx in the Bronx. It's a pretty big club."

"But how do you even know? I thought you didn't even know their name."

"Because while Mr. Groove Meister here was putting the moves on his new best buddy Joy the Hooker, I was making calls."

Mark smiles flatly. "Actually, that's Dr. Groove Meister, PhD, to you. And I wasn't putting the moves on her. I was teaching her the funky chicken."

Nikki smiles back. "And they say people with no soul can't dance."

Mark's jaw tightens. He storms out of the room.

I swallow. This is not how I want to be spending my final hours.

"Ted . . . um, sorry if I embarrassed you just now with the virginity stuff," Nikki whispers, avoiding my eyes.

"It's all right. But maybe you and Mark should work this out."

"What's to work out? I already know the funky chicken."

"Nikki, seriously—"

"Listen, I meant to tell you: Rachel called a bunch of times while you were out."

"She did?"

"Yeah. She left a few messages on the machine. It was hard to hear with all the music and everything, but I think she said she was sorry. Or something. I heard your cell phone ring a few times, too."

I glance at the nightstand beside my bed. Sure enough, my celly is sitting there, blinking. *Damn.* Why is Rachel apologizing? Why is she so nice? I should have called her first. I should have taken the phone with me to Billy Rifkin's. (But then, I should have done a lot of things. Like abstain from drinking Glenmorangie. Like get my stomach pumped . . .) If I'd taken the celly, though, I could have chosen the moral high ground for once, and apologized (it was my fault!), and settled things with Rachel a while ago—

Bee bee beep! Bee bee beep!

Right on cue, the celly starts ringing.

"Go ahead and answer," Nikki says, in barely a whisper.

"Take your time. I'll hail a cab for us. Hopefully Mark will come to his senses. But—"

Bee bee beep! Bee bee beep!

"But what?"

"There's just one thing I want to know. Did you really go see Billy Rifkin?"

"I did," I admit. "And . . ."

Bee bee beep! Bee bee beep!

". . . And he's not the same person he was before," I manage. "He's changed. So I didn't . . . I mean, I just didn't."

Our eyes meet once more, briefly. Nikki smiles. I see a glint of understanding. In those alien orbs, I see everything that's not said: that she knows I would never punch anyone in the face . . . and also that she feels bad about Mark, and that telling him he had no soul was unfair, and that she *doesn't* know the funky chicken. I want to tell her I understand. But I don't.

She scurries out of the room, closing the door behind her. Which probably says something, too. I'm just not sure what.

Trusting a Person Is All That Matters

I grab the phone and collapse on the bed. "Rachel?"

"Ted?" Her voice sounds tiny, as if she's calling from Bucharest.

"Listen, Rachel, I am so glad you called because—"

"Ted, I'm so sorry for storming off this afternoon."

"No, no. It wasn't your fault. It was my fault."

"What's all that noise?" she asks.

"What noise? You mean the static?"

"No, I hear music," she says. "Can you turn it down?"

"No!" I bolt upright and then quickly collapse again. The vertigo seems to be worsening. "I mean, no. You see . . . I was in the living room earlier. I was feeling really sick, you know? Music makes me feel better. So I turned on the stereo. Rachel, you have to understand: something really bad happened to me today."

"Ted, I know. I'm so sorry."

"No, I mean something *really* bad."

"Yeah, I understand. You got sick, and then you acted mean. I know I should have trusted you. I know I *can* trust you."

"Rachel, you have to listen—"

"Trusting a person is all that matters," she continues, but her signal is starting to break up. "You don't even drink! It's just that when I saw your shirt this afternoon and the way your face looked . . . I just . . . I'm sorry."

"It's fine, Rachel. I accept your apology. But look, did you see the news today?"

"Did you say the blues? Are you sad? Is this a guitar thing?"

"The news. Did you see it? Because—"

The bedroom door crashes open.

Joy stands before me, wagging a crystal decanter in front of her face. It's empty.

"Yo, sweetheart?" she squawks. "You got some more of this wine?" She spots the cell phone and clamps her free hand over her mouth. "Oh, damn, sorry!" she whispers. "That's your old lady, right?"

"Ted?" Rachel's voice rattles in my ear. "Is there somebody in your apartment right now?"

"Well, um . . ." *Damn it.* I can't lie now. I scowl at Joy as she staggers back out into the hall. (Isn't she supposed to know the meaning of discreet?) "Yeah, see, well, one of my parents' friends came to check up on me. My parents called her from Denver because they knew I was sick. It's Mrs. . . . It's Mrs. . . ."

I feverishly hunt for a name—and then a miracle occurs: For the second time tonight, I conjure a masterful lie out of thin air. (Is it possible that Leo's poison increases the brain's potential before killing you?) "It's Mrs. *Rifkin.* She came to check up on me. She's an old family friend. She's a really cool woman. She brought her checkbook, too."

"Her checkbook? I don't get it."

"She knows I'm involved in Amnesty International, so she made a two-hundred-dollar donation. She thought it would make me feel better."

There's silence on the other end.

"Rachel?"

"Ted, I don't believe you."

"You don't?"

"No. You're lying. I can tell. I can *always* tell when you're lying. Just like I can always tell when you're being honest. That's how I knew you were really sick today. But now . . . We were just talking about this! We were just talking about trust!"

Click.

"Rachel? Rachel?" I can't believe it. For the first time ever, Rachel has hung up on me. She's *that* mad. I stare up at the ceiling. I watch it rotate slowly, like a giant whirlpool. I should try to call her back. I should run over there right now. I should, I should . . . That's what this day is turning into, my "should" day. But I can't think about that right now. I have more pressing matters: namely, making sure that Mark gets Joy the hell out of here—*and* that he makes up with Nikki so we can all leave together. Because in spite of the fact that I feel terrible about Rachel, I'm suddenly filled with excitement.

I'm about to see Shakes the Clown!

Unbelievable. But I guess that's what happens when you're a sixteen-year-old music geek. That's what happens when you're an immature teenager who worships a bugged-out band. Even when you've just been a jerk to the one person who doesn't deserve it, you still fantasize about meeting these demented heroes of yours. Meeting them takes precedence over your own *girlfriend.*

Of course I would never, ever admit this to anyone because it's too ridiculous and loathsome. But at least I admitted it to myself for once. That's a start, right?

I toss the phone on the bed and stumble out to the living room.

Doughnut-Shaped Universe

Bad news: Nikki has just left the premises. She wasn't joking.

Worse news: Joy has decided to keep dancing, this time *on* the coffee table.

I can see scuff marks forming with every stomp and twist of her stiletto heels. She's helped herself to another bottle from the liquor cabinet, too—what looks like Jack Daniel's, although she's moving too fast and I'm too dizzy to tell for sure. She guzzles it straight. Mark crouches below her, snapping pictures with a Polaroid. I didn't know that he'd brought a camera. And actually . . . No, it's not his. I'm sure of this because somebody has rifled through the bureau where my parents keep *their* Polaroid. Drawers have been flung open. Old receipts are strewn everywhere.

"Yo, you got mad pictures up in this place!" Joy shouts at me, waving a hand at the walls in time to the music. "This place is crazy!"

Can't argue with that one. Nope. This place is crazy.

Mark whirls around and snaps a photo of me. I wince. The flash is blinding. Purple dots swim in front of my eyes. I stagger backward and fall into the couch.

"Let me take one!" Joy demands, hopping down.

Mark yanks the picture from the camera and tosses it on the floor, then lunges onto the couch, right on my lap.

"Oof," I grunt. "Stop it, Mark. Get off—"

Snap! There's another explosion of white light. I rub my watery eyes, grinning in spite of it all. Wait . . . am I having fun? I can't be. It's impossible. Nikki is seething with rage and waiting outside for me, Mark called a hooker—a hooker who seems determined to drain my parents' entire liquor cabinet—I've just been a total jerk and I'm dying of poison . . . but on the other hand, there's something fairly silly about all of this.

"Burger, we got a problem," Mark says, tumbling off my lap. He grabs the camera back from Joy and snaps one more of her. "I have to hang here until nine because that's when Joy's car service is coming to pick her up. So I'll catch up with you guys at Onyx. Okay?"

I blink a few times. "Uh—well, don't you think Joy can wait outside?" I smile at her. "I mean, no offense."

"None taken," she says. She crouches by the liquor cabinet, eyeing what's left.

"Why should she wait outside?" Mark asks.

DANiEL EHRENHAFT

"Because you should come with me and apologize to Nikki!" I shout.

"What for?" he says, as unfazed as ever. "I'll apologize when I get there."

"Mark, believe me. I know. You can't let an apology slip away—"

"Nikki's a big girl," he interrupts. "She'll be fine. She can take charge for a while. Hey, that reminds me! You better take this." He reaches into his pocket and pulls out the crumpled napkin. Since I saw it last, it's been stained with brown drops (scotch?), and two more tasks have been added—bringing the list to ten:

9. Start your own religion.
10. Get something named after you (like a park or a fountain).

"Uh . . . number nine might be a little tough," I tell him.

"Ah, you'll figure something out. How hard can it be? This is America, dude!"

I stuff the napkin into my own pocket, on top of Mrs. Rifkin's check. "What does America have to do with starting a religion?"

"People start their own religions all the time here, Burger!" he shouts. "Some of them blow up big, too. Look at the Mormons. The trick is to find a gimmick. Like a doughnut-shaped universe."

"Mark, how drunk are you right now?"

"No, no, no: listen. This is important because you don't have to worry about dying. I got it all figured out. See, a lot of physicists theorize that the universe is shaped like a giant doughnut, right? And if we could look hard enough . . . I mean, if we had the power to see across all of time and all of space and everything that has ever happened or ever will happen—we'd just end up looking around the entire doughnut and back at ourselves, at the back of our heads. Which makes sense, if you think about it. Because they say that God created us human beings in his image, you know? So if we could look at ourselves across all of eternity . . . in a way we'd be looking at God. But we couldn't see his *face*. We could only see the back of his head. Because you can never see the face of God, just like they say in the Bible. And you know what that *really* means? We never die. We're all part of the great big circle, and we're all part of eternity, and we're all a reflection of God. We don't disappear. We decompose and our atoms disperse and maybe we even become a part of something else—but we don't die. Get it?"

"Mark, you're hysterical. Why don't you just come with me?"

"I'll come in a second, okay?" He yanks me off the couch and escorts me into the foyer. The apartment spins around me. "Don't worry; I'll clean up here. And I'll get Joy out quick. I'll see you up at the Onyx." He hesitates for a second in front of the door. "Are we cool?"

"Mark—"

"Just get this list done for me, Burger," he says. "And take care of Nikki. Because if you don't, *I'm* gonna take you to the freaking hospital myself. Got it?"

Questions

I don't argue. I simply obey. Arguing is clearly bad. It's not how I should be spending the last hours of my life, as Mark and Nikki have proved.

Outside, Nikki has already hailed a taxi. She's waiting in the backseat, wringing her hands. I slide in beside her and shut the door.

"Brooks Avenue and 151st Street, the Bronx," she tells the driver. "Take the Willis Avenue Bridge. Thanks."

The driver guns the accelerator. We screech down the street. My head slams against the vinyl cushions. My stomach does a quick somersault. Another reason why I prefer mass transit to cabs: there's less chance of an accident on a subway. A subway ride is very smooth. Not so much starting and stopping, and fatalities, and—

Stop it. I refuse to think about death. I try to think about Shakes the Clown. I can't, though. Now that I'm *here*, alone with Nikki, all I can think about is what's going on *there*, back up in my apartment. I steal a few glances at her.

"Nikki, can I ask you something?"

"Sure," she says.

"Remember what you said earlier tonight? That I had to do something totally beyond the confines of morality? That I had to embrace the Dark Side? That I had to knock over a bank?"

"Yes, Ted," Nikki says dryly. "I was hoping you could be our vault man."

"Seriously, listen. I'm just saying: when Mark ordered Joy for me, didn't he embrace the Dark Side? Didn't he lead by example? By taking cash out on his parents' credit card to order a hooker for his friend? I mean, yes, he is an impulsive maniac—but still, that's not the kind of thing he does every day. Just like knocking over a bank isn't something that *you* do every day."

She smirks at me. "Are you sticking up for him?"

"I . . . uh—I, well, yeah. I guess I am."

"Why?"

"Because he would never hurt anybody on purpose! Especially you. He *does* have soul. Like the way he jumped in to save us today at the diner. Like with his dad and the whole dog thing. I mean, even just now, he went on this whole long rant about how I don't have to worry about dying because the universe is a giant doughnut . . . or something. I was sort of too dizzy to follow. The thing is, he's just really messed up right now, you know? He's taking this poison thing even worse than I am. *That's* soul."

Nikki sighs and turns away, gazing for a moment at the passing traffic. "You're something else, you know that?" she breathes. Then she turns back to me. "Can I ask *you* something?"

"Of course."

"Why don't we go to the hospital? Right now? Okay? Please?"

I laugh queasily. "Mark just said practically the same thing. That's what I mean."

"Well, he was being smart for once," she states. "So why don't we do it?"

Because I'm a coward! I'm terrified! Because I don't want to! Because I'd much rather go to a Shakes the Clown concert than think about it! (Forget the doctor; I need to see a shrink.) "Because I have to live life to the fullest, remember?" I reply casually. "I have to bungee jump off the GW Bridge. I mean, come on, Nikki. You said it yourself. Right?"

And I get the desired response: She laughs. It isn't much of a laugh, but it's a start. She looks as if she's about to add something.

"What?" I say.

"I don't know if it's my place to ask. It doesn't really have anything to do with . . . tonight. Well, no, that's not true. It has a lot to do with tonight."

"I don't have much time, Nikki," I joke lamely. "So you better ask away."

She stares at me from across the long gulf of the cab seat. "Have you been happy with Rachel? I mean these past few months, going out with her?"

"Have I . . ." *Wow.* I wasn't expecting that one.

Of course I've been happy with Rachel. I've been happy because I know what it's like not to have a girlfriend. I know what it's like to be horny and lonely. I know what it's like to sit across from a couple that is absolutely, completely, 100 percent in love, day in and day out. It's all I've ever known. On the other hand, I still am horny and lonely. And now it's looking like I'll die that way.

"Yes, I have been," I end up telling her. "I've been happy because she likes me."

Nikki laughs again.

"That's funny?" I ask.

"No, Ted. Sorry." She shakes her head sadly. "It's just, a lot of people like you. A lot of people *love* you. You know that? Ah—forget it. I really am sorry."

But I can't tell if she's sorry because she laughed or sorry because she implied that a lot of people love me. Unfortunately, she doesn't pursue it any further.

A Brief History of Shakes the Clown

So. Since wondering about my best friend's girlfriend's motives for asking me such a weird question isn't a whole of fun, I'd like to take a quick time-out here to tell you a little about my favorite band:

- The singer/guitarist and bassist (Hip E. Shake and Phurm Hand Shake, respectively[1]) met at the EZ-LERN Driving School in Brooklyn three years ago, when they were both sixteen.
- Both were music geeks, so they were naturally drawn to each other.[2]
- They were kicked out of class when they decided to spike their instructor's coffee with Manischewitz. (Their instructor, Mr. Firth, caught them in the act, an incident that was later memorialized in the song "Kosher Firth Day."[3])
- Not long after their expulsion from EZ-LERN, both discovered that they shared a love of the epic film *Shakes the Clown*, starring Bobcat Goldthwait.[4] They decided to renounce their previous identities, adopt stage names, forget about learning how to drive, and start a band named after the film.

---

1 Their real names are Wes Levitz and Herbert Goldstein.
2 Just take a look at their names. They aren't so far from Ted Burger.
3 It's on their first three-song demo: an impossible-to-find CD (but yes, I have it) called *Clowned Out*.
4 Hailed by one critic as "the *Citizen Kane* of alcoholic clown movies."

- They placed an ad in the *New York Press:* TWO LOSERS SEEKING DRUMMER FOR PURPOSES OF SCAMMING OLDER CHICKS. REQUIREMENTS: MUST BE AN OLDER CHICK OR HAVE PUNCHED A COP IN THE GROIN. MUST HAVE A CAR AND/OR VALID DRIVER'S LICENSE. MUST LOVE THE EPIC FILM *SHAKES THE CLOWN.* MUST ACCEPT TO BE CALLED BY A NEW NAME OF OUR CHOOSING. MUSICAL SKILLS A PLUS BUT NOT NECESSARY. NO PETS.[5]

- A twenty-year-old, six-foot, 180-pound, black female drummer with a five-inch Afro was the only person to respond to the ad. She met every single requirement. She agreed to be called "Sheik Down"[6] and joined immediately.

Thus the greatest band in the world was born.

An Overwhelming Urge to Lean Over and Hug Nikki

"What are you thinking about right now?"

Until Nikki said the words, I'd almost forgotten we were in the backseat of a taxi.

For a while now (I don't even know how long) my mind has

---

5 I have the original ad taped to my bedroom door.
6 Real name: Glenda Givens. She was training to be a cop until a fellow officer sexually harassed her, whereupon she punched him in the groin and quit. True story. I downloaded the police report.

been festering with questions—the questions I'd managed to stave off since she and Mark showed up at my door. As in: Why the hell *did* Leo poison the fries? Why would he kill the people who were loyal to him, who ate his product? Who else was poisoned? Should I notify the cops? File a report? Call my parents? *They don't even know yet!* Should I forget everything and finally take my friends' advice and just go to the stupid hospital? What would my parents say about what I'm doing right now?

"Ted?"

I take a deep breath. "I was thinking: I hope Shakes the Clown is good tonight."

She laughs softly. "That's really what you were thinking?" she says. Her black eyes glisten in the passing lights.

"No," I admit. "Well, sort of. I mean, this is the only time I'm ever gonna get to see them in my life, right? And they're my heroes. And I know that's lame and dorky, but it's true. So they better be good. What if they aren't as messed up as they make themselves out to be? What if they're a bunch of poseurs? What if they suck tonight?"

"They won't suck," Nikki says in a soothing voice.

"Yeah, but you see . . . Okay. I was really thinking about my parents. I was thinking about how they used to idolize Martha Stewart. I'm dead serious. They *worshiped* her. You know, before all the scandals and stuff? 'She's a brand identity unto herself!' they used to say. I mean, it was kind of twisted. They'd be staring at her on TV like they were watching the Pope or something, like a religious service. 'She's a genius, Ted! Just watch her!' And then, when all the allegations came out, they felt totally betrayed. It was like . . . she was a mirror to them. She reflected what they wanted to see in themselves. So when it turned out she wasn't perfect, they started *doubting* themselves. Because the mirror revealed these blemishes, you know?"

Nikki swallows.

"Ted, are you sure you're okay?" she asks. "I mean, how do you feel right now? How does your head feel?"

"Actually, it doesn't feel so bad. I mean, I feel weak and dizzy and nauseated, but it's not as bad as it's been."

"Oh," Nikki murmurs in a quavering voice. She turns toward the window.

I try to chuckle. She isn't going to start crying, is she? I wanted to lighten the mood. Time to change the subject. Or at least change it back.

"Look, I'm just saying that if Shakes the Clown sucks tonight, then that'll say something bad about me," I go on. "I'll spend the last hours of my life doubting myself. I swear. Because—and don't laugh—they embody Purity for me, with a capital *P*. They've never cared about anything except themselves. They've just played and played, and they've invented an entirely new joke-but-not-joke style of music. . . . They've had

DANIEL EHRENHAFT

the balls to do what I would never do. They've pursued their dreams at any and all costs. They always believed in their twisted agenda, and—well, now I'm starting to sound like I'm narrating a VH1 documentary. But it's true—"

"So in a way, they *can't* suck tonight," she gently interrupts.

"Huh?"

A sad little smile curls on her lips. "They can't suck, Ted. Even if they stumble off the stage piss-drunk, even if they refuse to play a single note . . . The thing is, you love them too much for them to suck. Just seeing them in person will be enough. Anything they do will make the show worthwhile. Anything."

I smile back. "You think so?"

"I *know* so. Ted, the whole point of having heroes is so you can look up to people who can get away with whatever they want. Because like you said, they've always had the courage to *do* whatever they want. Right?"

"I . . ." I bite my lip.

"What?"

"I was just thinking . . . Maybe, it sounds like you're talking about Mark?"

Nikki laughs bitterly. "Well, maybe Mark was my hero once," she says.

"He's not anymore?" I hear myself whisper.

"Ted, this is *your* night." She turns toward me, trying to act upbeat. "Let's not talk about my heroes. Let's talk about *yours*. Let's talk about how you're going to see Shakes the Clown in a few minutes, and party with them afterward, and jam all night into the wee hours. I'm serious. I'm gonna make this happen. I swear I will. The second we get there. Okay?"

I nod. "Okay."

I feel an overwhelming urge to lean over and hug her. But I don't. I simply turn back to my cab window, watching the East River as it rushes past.

We leave it at that.

Keep the Change

Maybe coming to this show tonight wasn't such a great idea.

Now that we've crossed the Willis Avenue Bridge, I remember why I don't make it up to the Bronx very often. It's a little sketchy. Sure, some parts are probably beautiful. I hear Riverdale is nice. But from what I can see right now (and this is just through a taxi window), the Bronx isn't like the other boroughs, even at their worst. It's got this sort of post-apocalyptic weirdness: deserted avenues littered with blown-out tires, old buildings where every single window is smashed, empty lots knee-deep in discarded bottles of Elmer's glue.

I mean, *Elmer's*? How desperate would you have to be to sniff Elmer's?

Clearly this neighborhood is not meant for Manhattan-bound wimps. Not by a long shot. I squint out into the night, trying to get some sense of where I am. Is Yankee Stadium out there? No. No, it isn't. All I see is a decrepit warehouse. *Wait* . . . A sign is mounted on the door. It's spray painted in black: THE ONYX.

So we're here. Wonderful. There's a big crowd outside, too. Mixed. Older. Rough looking. Lots of piercings and tattoos. All are bathed in a ghoulish white glow from a huge streetlamp overhead. (The industrial type, usually found in prison yards.) A few people stare at our taxi as it glides to a stop. None appear to be very pleased with its arrival.

"How much money do you have, Ted?" Nikki asks.

"Huh?"

She points to the meter. The fare is $25.80. "Don't worry," she says. "If you pay for the cab, I'll pay for the show. I'll charge the tickets on my credit card."

"Maybe it's sold out," I mumble. I fish through my pockets, cursing myself for not resisting the temptation to come up here. I should have gone straight to Rachel's apartment instead.

"It's not sold out," Nikki says. "I called ahead."

"Oh." I hand over the remainder of my cash: three crumpled ten-dollar bills.

Nikki thrusts the money at the driver and leaps out onto the sidewalk.

"Keep the change!" she calls over her shoulder.

I stagger after her. "Hey, Nikki, does this place even accept credit cards?"

But she's already halfway to the ticket booth, shoving her way through the crowd, a determined smile on her face. A girl with purple hair screams an obscenity at her. Nikki pretends not to hear. I turn and watch the cab as it disappears into the night. I can't help feeling that by letting it go, I've signed my own death warrant.

Of course, Leo already signed it for me.

The sidewalk starts to tilt. I tilt with it. I stare at a mishmash of gang-related graffiti on the club's cement wall, hoping that this will stabilize me. It doesn't. I suppose I should count my blessings, though. If I keel over and die right now, at least I'll have avoided a violent beating at the hands of—

"Forrest Chump!"

Freakin' Bold, Dude

No way.

It couldn't be. But I know it *is*, even before I spot the pair barreling toward me out of the mob. Lou and Frankie. The twins. There would be no mistaking those two dopey *Sopranos* accents, shouting in unison. Those two red baseball caps, worn backward. Those two sweatshirts, beer stained. The same sweatshirts, no less, with the same blue logos. Don't twins stop dressing alike after the age of three?

"Whattaya doin' here?" one of them yells at me.

I don't answer. A few thoughts flit through my mind. One: I hate that New York is the Land of Extraordinary Coincidence. Two: I can't tell who's who. (Does it even matter?) I don't understand how Rachel and these guys could have possibly been spawned by the same gene pool. There must have been a mix-up in the baby ward when Rachel was born. *She* doesn't speak with an accent. Plus she's not an ape. I'm also thinking: she was right. Drunks do appear to suffer from the same symptoms I do. Their cheeks bloat; their eyes redden; their gait is unsteady.

"I thought you were at home sick," the other says, breathing beer into my face. *Tawt yoo wurr at 'ome sick.*

Hmmm. What are they going to think when Nikki gets back here with the tickets? Actually, I know the answer. They're going to think that I'm cheating on their sister.

"That's freakin' *bold*, dude," one says.

"What?"

"That you busted it!" the other one cries.

My eyes flash between them. I can no longer tell if I'm in any immediate danger. Neither twin's tone is overtly threatening. Are they setting me up?

"You must really dig Rachel," the first one says.

"Of course I do!" I reply instantly. My voice squeaks. I try to smile.

They laugh.

"I'mma go get her," the other one slurs, lurching back toward the club. "Cuz, you know, we were thinking about lookin' you up and beatin' the snot outta you. She told us you lied to her. Big-time."

My smile disappears. Blood pools in my feet.

"She's here?" I gasp.

"Yeah, she felt sorta bad about comin' and all," the remaining twin says. "I mean, seein' as you were sick. She was gonna surprise you with the ticket. She bought two. You know, one for her, one for you. But then she was like, why waste two tickets? I mean, you know Rachel, dude. Waste not, want not! So she gave it to Lou. And I bought one here. She's always wanted to see this band 'cuz you're always talking about 'em—and by the way, I LOVE SHAKES THE CLOWN, DUDE! They're just like . . . just like . . . you know?" He belches, frowning. "Wait, what was I saying?"

Things I Love About Rachel Klein, Redux

I'm about to start sniffling again. I'm about to break down and bawl like I did on the subway home from Billy Rifkin's. I stare up at Frankie's beefy red face—it has to be Frankie because he mentioned Lou—and I want to throw my arms around him. (On second thought, I don't want to do that.) But I want to hug *somebody*. I want to hug his sister. Because during his semi-coherent monologue, I ran the entire emotional gamut: from fear, to guilt, to shock, to understanding, to happiness, to more guilt, then to *more* . . . . and finally I wound up with remorse.

I *do* love Rachel Klein.

What's not to love? In no particular order:

1. She respects my opinion.
2. She respects it so much that she wanted to see Shakes the Clown herself.
3. She bought *me* a ticket to see it with her. She wanted to surprise me. Me! The guy who runs away! The guy who blows stuff off!
4. She *knows* me. She knew I'd be overjoyed with her offer to take me to this show. She's warm and generous and caring and beautiful and—

Here she comes.

Well Done

"See?" Lou drags her out of the crowd by the entrance and shoves her toward me. Her sandals crunch on broken glass. "I told you he was here."

Rachel freezes. "Ted?" she cries.

"Uh, that's the name they gave me," I say, with horrible bad-clown timing.

She gapes at me in the heinous fluorescent Bronx streetlight. I can't get a bead on what she's feeling. Is she suspicious? Relieved? Still pissed? Strange: even as my brain squirms, I find myself glancing back toward the ticket window, where Nikki has been out of sight for some time. There isn't really a line; it's more of an unruly mob. Even so, I'm sure that Nikki has managed to buy us tickets by now. She'll probably return at any second. At which point I'll be forced to admit to Rachel that I came to the Onyx with Nikki, alone—just the two of us—to see my favorite band.

"What are you doing here?" she finally asks.

"I came with Mark," I lie, without a moment's hesitation.

"Oh," she says.

I start feeling sick. What the hell was that? Actually, I know the answer to *this* moronic rhetorical question, too. I was looking to stall her. Of course I was. I still am. I'm looking for anything to postpone having to tell Rachel the truth. And until the very moment Nikki appears with the tickets, I'll have bought myself some time. I'll have survived a few more seconds without making Rachel miserable. It was just a basic animal instinct, the instinct for survival and protection. A reflex. Like throwing up when you're nauseated—

Uh-oh.

DANiEL EHRENHAFT

I throw up, with sudden violence.

"DUUUUUDE!" the twins cry in disgust. They back off toward the club.

A couple of people snicker.

"Shuddup!" Lou and Frankie bark at them.

"Ted?" Rachel says, very gently. She wraps her arm around me and bends down. Her eyebrows meet in a soft arc. "Look. I know I asked you this earlier, but have you been drinking?"

"Yeah," I confess. At this point I'm too miserable to lie anymore.

"When did you start?"

"I started at my apartment. But listen." I take a deep breath and stand up straight. Amazingly, I feel much better. I've also avoided ruining my shirt this time. I run a hand through my damp curls. I steady myself enough to explain what's really going on, to be honest, and to tell her that getting drunk earlier has nothing to do with this. "I've been meaning to tell you something. This afternoon I was—"

"Please don't tell me that you've come down with some weird sickness, Ted," Rachel pleads. "I forgive you, okay? And I'm sorry I hung up on you earlier. But please don't lie to me. Please don't make up any more BS about how some friend of your parents' came to check up on you and she gave you a two-hundred-dollar donation to Amnesty International. . . ."

Wait—that's right. I have proof of my innocence. My face

lights up with the same joy that Dad's did when he first told me about the Napkin. "No, no, Rachel, look," I protest. I jam my fist into my pocket and yank out the crumpled check. The spring break/death mission/ten things list pops out with it, fluttering to the sidewalk. But I don't care. In sniveling fashion, all I care about is the immediate moment. About exonerating myself. "See? I wasn't making that up."

Rachel steps forward. She plucks the check from my hand with her heavily calloused, gardening-scarred fingers. Her eyes widen.

"Oh my God," she breathes.

I resist the urge to pump my fist in the air. *Yes! Victory! Everything's coming up Burger!* I snatch up the list and stuff it back into my pocket. My head spins with the bending over. I should probably avoid doing that again.

"What's that?" Rachel asks.

"What's what?"

"That thing you just picked up. That napkin."

"Oh. It's nothing."

"It looks like something was written on it."

"Yeah, you know—just . . . stuff." I shrug and smile, blushing. I wanted to tell her about the poisoning, but now I can't. There's no telling how she would react if she saw that list in all its madness. I would have to explain why I'm not in the hospital. I would have to explain why I'm here with Nikki. I would have to tell more lies. . . .

But she just smiles back. *Incredible.* She's in such a forgiving mood, she decides not to be nosy. "Look, Ted, I don't want to sound like a nag or your mother or anything, but don't you think you should go home and get into bed? It probably wasn't such a great idea to drink when you weren't feeling well, you know? I'll call you a cab right now." She reaches into her sweater for her cell phone. "Where's Mark, by the—"

"Getting the tickets!" I interrupt.

I scan the crowd near the ticket window. (Still no sign of Nikki.) I scan the twins. (Nothing there, no hint of any emotion or comprehension whatsoever.) Then I scan Rachel. (Sadness and sympathy.) I make the loop again. A third time. Crowd, twins, Rachel; crowd, twins, Rachel; crowd . . . That brief, euphoric exultation vanishes. Despair replaces it. I've woven a very tenuous web of deceit for myself, and now it's on the verge of unraveling.

Well done, Ted, I congratulate myself grimly. *Very well done.*

"Ted?"

"Yes?"

Rachel looks at me. And then she does something that should make me feel extremely relieved but doesn't. It makes me feel about as bad as I've felt since this whole ordeal started.

She sweeps me into her arms for a hug.

"I know how excited you are to see this show," she murmurs into my ear. "And I'm sorry. But I really think it's best if you go home."

"Rachel?"

"Yeah?"

"We need to talk." I step away from her and take her lumber-jack hand. I can tell she sees an uncharacteristic sobriety in my bloodshot eyes. She senses that what I'm about to say is impor-tant. And she's right because even though *I* don't know what I'm about to say—not word for word—I've just had a minor revela-tion. I've just gone from loving her more than I ever have, to . . . well, to still loving her, in a way. Except now I know what I have to do. I have to make another speech. A tough one, along the same lines of the speech I made on the subway. It's been build-ing. It was building even before I discovered I was poisoned. The hug triggered it, though. That hug was the final blow.

"What's up, Ted? What is it?"

My fingers intertwine with hers.

"Come with me," I say. I lead her away from the crowd, away from the offensive glare of the streetlamp, away from Lou and Frankie (and Nikki, too)—around the corner to a deserted side street, littered with blown-out tires.

"I . . ." I search for a delicate phrase. "I don't like feeling guilty all the time."

She laughs uncomfortably. "What do you mean?"

"You make me feel guilty."

"I do?" Her lips quake. Her forehead wrinkles. She wraps her arms tightly around herself. Her oversized wool sweater sleeves hang limply over her hard little fingers. She stares down at her sandals.

Way to go, Ted, I tell myself angrily. Now she's hurt. Why did I say that? It wasn't just blunt; it was cruel. I wanted to spare her feelings. But given that outburst of stupidity, sparing her feelings probably won't be an option now. My guilty conscience is *my* problem, not hers.

"What are you trying to tell me, Ted?" she whispers, glancing up again.

"I don't know. I'm sorry, Rachel. But really, what do you get out of this?"

"What do I get out of *what*? Ted, you're not making any sense. I'm worried about you."

"I know you are," I say. It's crazy: as we both stand here in this godforsaken wasteland, I start trying to dream up ways of tricking her into getting mad at me—so *she'll* take the initiative to break up with me tonight, so *I* won't have to feel guilty about not wanting to spend the last few hours of my life with her. Which, of course, just makes me feel guiltier. What could I possibly say or do to make her mad at me? Tell her that I lied to her? Tell her that I came here with Nikki, alone?

"Ted, I'm calling a car service for you," she says. She flips open her celly. "You won't even have to pay for it. My parents have an account at Tribeca Limos. It'll be here in a half hour, tops. You can go home, and rest, and wake up early, okay?"

She punches a few buttons and cradles the phone against her ear.

This is it. This is the time to *do* it. I have to swallow my fear. I can't afford to blow things off anymore. It's better for Rachel in the long run. It'll spare her—

"Yeah, hi!" Rachel says. She shifts on her feet, smiling absently at a nearby pile of tires. "Account number two-three-eight-nine? Yes. Klein." She pauses. "I'll need a car to pick up one passenger at the Onyx in the Bronx. Brooks Avenue and 151st Street." She flashes me a quick grin and nods. "Car four-ten? Great! No, not cash. Voucher. The passenger's name is Burger. Ted Burger. Right. He's going to Barrow Street in Manhattan. Thanks!" She snaps the phone shut. "So, Ted . . ."

Before she can say another word, I turn and bolt.

A Really Huge Favor

The sidewalk veers sharply down to the left as I hurry back around the corner toward the club entrance. But I've grown accustomed to such hallucinations. I can compensate by leaning in the opposite direction. Good for me.

I'm a real champ.

This is it. I've sunk far below sniveling cowardice. There's no term for what I just pulled back there. It wasn't just "escape." It wasn't just my usual MO. It . . . *Christ.* Forget it. I can't think about it anymore. It'll ruin my last twenty poisoned hours on earth. Which deserve to be ruined. I will say this: I definitely have embraced the Dark Side. Well . . . maybe not so much Dark as Slimy, Cruel, Selfish, and Shallow.

The crowd outside the Onyx has grown exponentially, like a virus, just during that brief minute or so. It fuels my depression, in a way. It tells me that Shakes the Clown is no longer strictly underground. They've moved up. They're *trendy* now. I doubt all these people really love them. Not the way I do. I have the bootlegs to prove the love, going all the way back. But I can't think about *that* now, either. No, I need to focus on putting as much distance as possible between me and Rachel Klein and, by extension, between me and Lou and Frankie Klein as well.

Thankfully, the twins are nowhere to be seen.

I squirm into a mass of bodies. I also try my best not to anger anybody. It doesn't work. Under normal circumstances I can be invisible but not here: I'm sweaty and stinky and I'm the only one who doesn't have a tattooed neck or pierced eyelid. I catch a few elbows, some glares, snippets of threats, a gathering storm of outlaw viciousness directed solely at me. But I console myself once more with the knowledge that if I'm beaten to a bloody pulp, I'll have *escaped.* I'll have escaped it all.

"Burger!"

Oh God, no.

"Burger! BURGER, dude!"

The color drains from my face. If Mark is here, it's only a matter of time before he draws attention to me and Rachel finds me, too, and the truth gets spilled. . . . *How did he get here so fast?* I squeeze my eyes shut in a last-ditch effort to flee reality. But there is no fleeing. When I open my eyes back up, Mark is standing right in front of me. He's also as wild-eyed and sweaty as ever. His GIVE THIS DAWG A BONE T-shirt is practically soaked through.

"What's up?" he says, gasping for breath. "Where's Nikki?"

"She . . . uh—she went to get tickets." I swallow, glancing over both shoulders. A couple of people jostle him. He doesn't bat an eyelash. "It's a pretty crazy scene here, huh? You know, it cost me thirty bucks to get here by cab."

"Me too. So what happened with Joy?"

"She split maybe ten minutes after you guys did. It was tough getting her out of the apartment, but I forced the issue. I cleaned up a little bit, too." He starts grinning. "Well, not so much. But a little bit."

"Oh." I chew my lip. "Listen, Mark, I need you to do me a really huge favor."

DANIEL EHRENHAFT

He laughs. "I just spent four hundred bucks to get you laid. That doesn't cut it?"

"I'm serious!"

"Okay, okay. Hey, look, I'm sorry if I bummed you out with the hooker thing—"

"It's okay," I interrupt. "But look, I need to split. And I need you to find Rachel. She was right around the corner the last time I saw her."

"Whoa. Wait. Rachel is *here*?"

"Yeah." I cast another anxious glance over the crowd. "But when you find her, I need you to tell her that you and I came here together, all right? And that I wasn't feeling well so I had to go home. Right away. I couldn't wait around for her car service. And that even though we were drinking earlier today, I really *am* sick. Got it?"

Mark blinks at me a couple of times. "No. I don't 'got it.'"

"Just do it."

"Do what? If Rachel is here, why don't you just talk to her?"

"I tried! But she wouldn't let me break up with her, all right?"

His eyes start to narrow. "She wouldn't . . . *let* you?"

"No! She wouldn't!"

"Burger, I think we should all leave. I think we should forget about this show and get you to the goddamn hospital. I think . . ." He doesn't finish.

"You think what?"

At that moment his face goes slack—the way it often does when he thinks he has a stroke of genius—and his gaze fixes squarely on something (or someone) behind us. I spin around.

It's Nikki.

"Hi, Mark," she says.

"Hi, Nikki," he says.

There's nothing between them. No long, meaningful exchange. They hardly even look at each other.

"Ted, you're coming with me," she announces. She grabs my arm and yanks me away from him without so much as another glance in his direction. Her ringed fingers dig into the flesh above my elbow. She slices through the mob, fearlessly, toward an unmarked door several yards from the entrance.

"Where are we going?" I ask her.

"To meet Shakes the Clown," she says.

The Indescribable Feeling You Get When Your Real Life Exceeds Your Dreams

The words don't register at first.

"Sorry, what was that?"

"You heard me." She drags me the last few feet to the door, then turns and flashes a quick smile. "Are you psyched?"

DANIEL EHRENHAFT

"Am I . . ."

"Don't answer." She knocks in a deliberate, even rhythm, as if she's tapping out code. Several of the more heavily pierced crowd members watch her. My pulse skips a beat. These people could do anything right now: stab us, pull a gun—*anything*. And I'd be powerless to stop them. Then again, what difference would my murder make? It would only hasten the inevitable. I stand there, mute in Nikki's clutches, feeling vaguely like a convict who's being transferred from one penitentiary to another.

"Who is it?" a muffled voice asks from inside.

"Nikki," she says.

The door swings open. A pale arm slithers out of the darkness and latches on to her, dragging us both inside.

Slam!

For a moment it's pitch-black.

Then a lightbulb flickers.

I find myself standing beside an emaciated kid with spiky black hair and dead green eyes. Eyes that are almost as familiar to me as my own. He's wearing leather pants and a white wife-beater undershirt, on which he's scrawled I'M WITH STUPID in red marker. Below these words he's drawn a sloppy arrow, pointing straight down to his crotch.

Wes Levitz. Aka Hip E. Shake.

My hero.

Okeydokey, Artichokey?

"So, who's the skirt?" Hip E. Shake asks Nikki.

The skirt?

He turns to me and bursts out laughing.

The vortex inside my head swirls at full throttle. Thoughts bounce around like popcorn in a microwave. *He and Nikki know each other!* (How did that happen?) *Nikki must have told him about me!* (But what did she tell him?) *He already hates my guts!* (He called me a . . . skirt?)

"Well, he's not much to look at," Hip E. Shake says.

Nikki doesn't react.

I try to smile. I can manage only a sickly grin.

"Ah, I'm just clowning you." He punches me on the arm, hard. Then he smiles, revealing a mouthful of gold teeth. The top row spells $I$$Y. This is new, as far as I know. "So, you've been poisoned and got twenty-four hours left. Is that right?"

My grin fades.

"Yeah," Nikki pipes up, assuming the role of spokesperson. "Did you see it on the news today? It was the fry cook at the Circle Eat Diner."

"I don't watch the news," Hip E. Shake says. "I only watch porn."

"Oh." Nikki frowns. "Well. Anyway, like I said, you guys are his favorite band. So he wanted to meet you before, you know, he . . ."

"Before he croaks," Hip E. Shake finishes.

Her frown hardens. "That's right."

"And your name is Tad, right?" he asks.

I nod, unable to speak.

"Actually, it's *Ted*," Nikki snaps.

Hip E. Shake nods thoughtfully. "Hey, sister, I understand where you're coming from." He lowers his voice, breathing the same stale beer stink into my face that Lou and Frankie did. "You see, I was born into poverty. My mother named me Lester. Les for short. You know, since we had 'less' than most people. But she has a speech impediment. It came out sounding like 'Wes.' Sadly, it stuck. And I've been a widdle ang-wee ever since. So I'd like you to call me Wes. Or Wester. Nothing else. Otherwise I'll cut you up wike the wox at Zabar's. Okeydokey, artichokey?"

In Order of Importance

What happens next is a little foggy.

Hip E. Sha—sorry, Wes—leads us down a long and dimly lit cement corridor, but that's basically all I'm conscious of. I'm still grappling with a variety of issues and unanswered questions. In order of importance (at least, for the moment):

1. How did Nikki arrange for me to meet Shakes the Clown?

2. My hero is a psychopath.

3. Mark and the three Klein siblings are outside, separately waiting to see the show. Have they run into each other yet?
4. Has Rachel found out about what Leo did to me?
5. I'm hungry. I haven't eaten all day, except for poisoned fries.
6. What if I puke again?
7. The show was supposed to start at 9 p.m. It's already 9:17.

Myself, Ted Burger

If there's an appropriate way to behave around famous people, I haven't seen it yet. Granted, the members of Shakes the Clown aren't exactly famous. (And granted, I've never hung around famous people in the first place.) But from what I've gleaned off TV, there are generally three types of behavior. (1) There's the sycophantic: *"Yes, Mr. Rock Star, I'll be getting those slippers for you right away!"* (2) There's the inner circle wannabe: *"So, Mr. Rock Star, after the show tonight let's ditch these hangers-on and go to that bar we snuck into in the eighth grade because I knew you before you were famous and we're lifelong buddies, right?"* (3) There's the purposefully aloof: *"I'm going to ignore you, Mr. Rock Star, because you're just another human being, and I could easily do what you do, so the truth is, you make me sick."*

DANIEL EHRENHAFT

So when Wes crashes through a door marked AUTHORIZED PER-SONNEL ONLY (protected by a mountain of a bouncer who makes the obese security guard at St. Vincent's look like a famine victim), I make a mental note not to behave in any of those ways. I'm just going to be myself. Ted Burger. *Appropriately* sycophantic. *Not* part of the inner circle. *Too* sycophantic to be aloof.

It should be easy. All I have to do is stand there like a dope. I've had plenty of practice doing that.

Human Sacrifice

The AUTHORIZED PERSONNEL ONLY door opens on a stuffy green-tiled cell. It's approximately the size and shape of a gas station restroom. It smells like a gas station restroom, too, except there are no toilets. There are no furnishings at all, aside from a battered vinyl seat, which appears to have been torn out of a van or minibus.

In my wild daydreams I've always imagined backstage areas to be glamorous and over the top—loaded with catered sushi and lighted mirrors, beautiful groupies, rampant sex . . . a seething den of iniquity and mayhem, dripping with unseen cash. Was I wrong? Where's the champagne? The hors d'oeuvres? Spreadwise, I see only a rusted bucket full of canned Budweiser. And there are no groupies, aside from a pasty guy in a flannel shirt. He's standing over the other band members, Phurm Hand Shake and Sheik Down, who slouch together on the vinyl seat, silently nursing beers. That's it. There aren't even any other people in the room.

Phurm Hand Shake is squirrelly. Literally. Much more so than I remember him in the photos on their official Web site. He's got the same frizzed-out dull brown hair, and he's hunched over his beer the way a squirrel would hunch over an acorn, picking at the label. His yellow buckteeth hang over his lips. He has no neck, either—just a long, flaccid chin that seems to extend from the bottom of his face to the top of his tattered AC/DC concert T-shirt. He's also wearing a kilt.

Sheik Down is a lot more imposing in person than she is on the site. She's easily a foot taller than Phurm Hand Shake, even sitting down. She sports big bug-eye sunglasses and a gaudy denim suit: lots of silver snaps and Nashville-style embroidery. In fact, she reminds me a little of Lenny Kravitz, but only if Lenny Kravitz decided to turn country and get a sex change.

The pasty guy starts running his mouth: "What I'm saying is, Wicked Records *gets* you. We understand your thing. You're smart-stupid. Am I right? You know? Like sexy-ugly? Like if I could sum you up in a gag, it would be when a piano drops on a guy's head, and the guy turns out to be a piano tuner? Smart-stupid, right? You think a major label would get that? And if you sign Wicked Records, as in now, *tonight,* we can guarantee you distribution that no other independent label can. . . ."

"How did this happen?" I whisper to Nikki.

"How did *what* happen?" she whispers back.

"How did you get me backstage? How did you meet these guys?"

She lifts her shoulders. "It's not that hard to meet a band if you're a chick. I flirted with the bouncer. I gave him my number."

"You *did*?"

"Actually, I gave him Mark's number." She winks at me. "But the bouncer doesn't know that."

". . . with the proper marketing—"

"Twig?" Wes calls, silencing the guy in the flannel shirt. "Can you come here for a minute, please?"

An instant later the bouncer appears in the doorway. (Nine hundred pounds and his name is Twig?) He's so huge that he practically has to ooze into the room, as if via osmosis. "Yeah?" he grunts.

"Our little flannel friend has had too much beer," Wes says. "It's making him talk funny."

Twig grins. "You want me to dismantle him?"

"Yes, I do, please," Wes says. "I'd go with a Mayan flavor. Human sacrifice." He turns to the guy in the flannel shirt. "Or is that not 'smart-stupid' enough?"

"Hey, what's your problem?" the guy says. He backs away, glancing around the room. "What did I do?"

"You have a severe case of diarrhea of the mouth," Wes says. "Now it's time to get constipated."

"I'm your one-ton barrel of Imodium," Twig says, stepping toward him.

The guy's face turns paler. Suddenly he hightails it straight past Twig—down the hall, through the door, and out into the street.

"Mayan Imodium!" Twig yells after him.

Wes giggles. So do his bandmates.

Nikki is starting to look antsy. I'm filled with anger. Not at her, of course, but at these morons. I'm no longer feeling detached enough to appreciate their absurdity. I feel like asking them a few questions. Like, oh, say: Why are you so violent and immature? Why would you threaten a guy who was trying to offer you a record deal, even if he did talk too much? A deal with an independent label, no less? It wouldn't even be selling out! True, the guy was foolish and annoying. But he was right. He articulated exactly what *I've* maintained from the moment I discovered you: You *are* (for lack of a better term) smart-stupid. So why didn't you recognize his gibberish for what it was? Namely: a huge compliment? Why don't you *care*? Most important, why are you deliberately trying to freak Nikki and me out? Forget the questions; I want to slap all of you.

But I don't say a word, of course. I just stand there like a dope.

Contagious Electricity

"Tad, we understand you have a list of some kind," Wes says.

"Um . . ."

"Hand it over," he commands.

My shaky fingers plunge into my pocket. I force another idiotic laugh. I should really grab Nikki and get the hell out of here.

Wes snatches the crumpled napkin from me. "Let's see," he muses. "Number one: lose virginity." He glances up. "How'd that go for you? Yay? Nay?"

My stomach twists. The room starts to spin. After a brief intermission Death has suddenly returned center stage. I wonder what it would feel like to beat the crap out of my hero. Probably pretty good. (A hell of a lot better than punching Billy Rifkin, for sure.) I don't know if I could get a decent jab in, though. I'm too dizzy.

Wes scratches his flat stomach for a second. Then he turns to Sheik Down. "Glenda, will you have sex with Tad?"

She slurps her beer. "I'm a lesbian," she says. "Remember?"

"No, I don't, but I'll trust you on that." He glances back down at the napkin. "So that brings us to number two. Jam with Shakes the Clown." He clucks his tongue. "Hey, man, you're so lucky that you're dying. We don't let just anyone chill with us."

"Just shut up and let him play for you, all right?" Nikki snaps. "You told me you would. If you aren't going to, then I'd like to leave."

The room falls dead silent.

But just like that, Wes is no longer angry. His dead green eyes dance with electricity. And the electricity is contagious. Herbert and Glenda leap to their feet. The whole room springs to life. *Happy* life. They've suddenly become like the giddy little elves you see on cookie commercials. The three of them hoot and applaud.

"Get a load of this clown!" Wes exclaims, slapping Nikki affectionately. "This chick has some serious balls. And she's right!" He points to me. "Ted Burger, this is your life. And death. The time has come to prove yourself."

He tosses the napkin on the floor and hurries out of the room.

I turn to Nikki, speechless.

She sneaks one last quick wink at me while nobody's looking. And I want to hug her more than ever. Because I realize exactly what I love about my best friend's girlfriend: Nikki can communicate a whole night's worth of insanity without having to utter a single word. She never gets diarrhea of the mouth.

Not many people are like that.

DANIEL EHRENHAFT

The Magnificent Balloon Rhinoceros Analogy

Wes returns with a guitar in one hand and a tiny practice amp in the other.

"Let's see what you're made of," he says, nearly tripping on the cord connecting the two. He shoves the guitar at me. "Let's see it, Ted Burger."

Now, *this* is insane. Sure, I've fantasized about such a scenario a million times. But this is the guitar that Wes Levitz had custom built. I recognize it instantly from their fan site: it's bright purple and shaped like a banjo. He never lets anybody touch it.

I wonder if he's setting me up for a beating.

"Take the guitar," he orders.

I obey. What choice do I have? I strap it over my shoulders. Wes cradles the little amp against his bony chest, fiddling with a few of the knobs. He pulls a pick out of his leather pocket. It's emblazoned with a tiny picture of Bobcat Goldthwait's face.

"Now, rock," he concludes.

Rock?

Well, beating or not, at least I can already tell that playing this guitar is going to be a joy. I take the pick and light right into "Kosher Firth Day." (It begins with a heavy, distorted, ascending riff: a thinly veiled takeoff on Led Zeppelin's "Heartbreaker.") My fingers fly over the fret board. The strings bend and shriek at my every whim. Compared to *my* piece of crap electric guitar . . .

No, there is no comparison. This is the best guitar I've ever played. The action is low, the intonation is perfect, and there isn't a hint of buzz.

I know that probably doesn't mean much unless you play guitar, too—but imagine it this way. Imagine you're a professional clown. A big part of your act is making balloon animals. For years you've worked with the same cheap and unforgiving balloons. They always pop. (Always at the worst times, too. Always when the birthday boy or girl is whining for one.) Then one day you find a new brand of super-strong, super-elastic balloons. Not only are they impossible to pop, you can finally twist up the magnificent balloon rhinoceros—which you've never even *tried* before. But now you can pull it off without breaking a sweat, and the birthday boy or girl is overjoyed at the sheer size and beauty and indestructibility of it . . . and, well, you get the point.

That's basically how I feel right now.

Give This Man a Clown Nose!

"Hey! Schmucks!"

It's Twig. He's back in the doorway, glaring at us.

154   DANiEL EHRENHAFT

Whoops. I turn the volume knob down. How long have I been playing? I don't even know.

"You were supposed to go on a half hour ago," he says.

Wes rolls his eyes. "I was supposed to do a lot of things, Twig. Wasn't I? Like finish driver's ed? Like go to college, the way my nana wanted. . . . Oh, never mind." He jabs a finger in my face. "Ted Burger, are you some kind of autistic savant?"

I swallow. "Am I what?"

"See, that's what I'm talking about. It might be the poison, but you strike me as retarded. Yet you play much better than I do. You play my own songs better than I play them myself. It's a problem for me."

I glance at Nikki. She winks again.

"WES!" Twig snarls. "Get onstage! NOW!"

Wes gives him the finger.

"Ted Burger must gig with us," Herbert proclaims.

"Ted Burger must gig with us tonight," Glenda concurs.

"So get him up there, already," Nikki mumbles.

"Yes!" Wes yanks the cord from the guitar and tosses the practice amp into the bucket of beer. It lands with a cannonball splash. "Give this man a clown nose!"

Again, I'm a little too overstimulated to get a good handle on what comes next. It's all pretty rapid-fire. Twig exits the room. The band members descend upon me. Glenda produces a rubber clown nose and straps it to my face from behind. Wes produces a red Magic Marker and scribbles the words *Shake 'n Bake* on my T-shirt. Herbert produces a beer and pours a few drops over my head, as if baptizing me.

"Shake 'n Bake," the three of them chant, with mystical zeal.

"It's a dumb name, Ted Burger," Wes says. "But we're a little pressed for time."

Glenda takes my arm and whisks me to the door.

I can see how she would have made a good cop. Her powerful fingers dig into the same sore spot where Nikki grabbed me just minutes ago. Herbert and Wes follow. I catch a last glimpse of Nikki. She's picking the napkin off the green tile—cautiously, with her thumb and forefinger, as if she's worried the filthy floor might contaminate her. I want to tell her to forget about the stupid napkin, but it's too late; I'm already marching briskly through a labyrinth of dim corridors. Along the way ghostly figures hand the band members various instruments: Wes, a guitar (also purple, though not banjo shaped); Herbert, a bass; Glenda, her drumsticks. . . .

We hurry up a stairwell. . . .

Blackness.

I hear a massive, hollow, cacophonous buzz: the kind that indicates vast space and hundreds of people packed tightly together. Then there's a light. A lone flashlight beam. It dances over amplifiers, a drum kit—and for a nightmarish instant, a sea of faces.

The stage? I'm onstage!! Holy—

My mouth dries up. I can't breathe. (The clown nose doesn't help.) My heart starts to thump like that rap song Joy and Mark were listening to earlier. How the hell did I get here? Not that it matters because I'm certain the poison will send me toppling to the floor—

"Where should he plug in?" somebody whispers.

Twig? Is that you?

I can't tell. I can't see a goddamn thing.

"Plug him into the acoustic rig," Wes whispers back, sounding oddly professional. "It should be fine. We dealt with it in the sound check. We'll get him off after the first song. Herbert and I can stall for time."

Glenda suddenly lets go of me.

"Hey!" I protest. "Come back!"

Her grip was viselike, but I preferred the pain because at least then I was anchored somewhere. Now I'm just *out here,* blind, a free-floating entity in the final preshow chaos, the crucial word being *show,* a show I have no legitimate part of . . .

The flashlight zooms into my face. I flinch, covering my eyes.

I sense that somebody is bending down next to my groin.

There's a *click.* Whoever's down there just plugged my guitar in. When my fingers accidentally brush over the strings—mostly in an attempt to get this mystery person (boy? girl? man? woman?) away from my private parts—I produce the loudest, most horrific noise I've ever heard: *Beeeow!*

It echoes across the club: *Beeeow . . . beeeow . . . beeeow . . .*

A cheer erupts in response: *"Woooooo!"*

No. My blood runs cold. *No. No!* That wasn't some kind of signal! But the sound is overpowering. It's a wall, a force—I can *feel* it.

"You ready to lose your Shakes the Clown virginity?" Wes whispers out of nowhere. "Are you ready to get stupid-smart, Ted Burger?"

Am I ready?

"'Kosher Firth Day' on four," he instructs me. Seconds later his voice booms from a microphone: "One, two, three, four—"

The Answer to Wes's Question

Before we get to all that, there's something you should know:

I've never performed in front of a formal audience, except for one other time in my life. In other words, until this very moment, the only time I've ever actually stood on a stage while people watched me—and this is the God's honest truth—was at a school assembly in the sixth grade, when I sang "If I Were a Rich Man" from the musical *Fiddler on the Roof.*

That's it.

It also bears mentioning that the performance was a disaster. I can't carry a tune. So I spent the whole time staring at Mark—he was in the fourth row—and he cringed and tried to smile as I struggled through the entire song, painfully off-key. I sweated a lot. Needless to say, Mom and Dad wasted an entire roll of film on this hellish torture. Many of the pictures still hang on our apartment wall.

But as far as the guitar goes? Nope. Never played it in public. Nor have I particularly desired to. The prospect has always been too frightening. I've never auditioned for a band. I've never played with any other musicians. Not with a drummer, not with a singer, not with a bassist, not with any combination thereof. I've never even played with any other *human beings*—except Mr. Puccini. And Rachel, I guess, if you count one miserable attempt we made to "jam" before . . . well, before.

So.

What I'm trying to say is: no, Wes Levitz, aka Hip E. Shake—in answer to your question, no. I am not "ready" to lose my Shakes the Clown virginity.

Ha! Sound familiar?

Note to self before dying: If I ever make up with Rachel, I will never bug her about consummating our relationship again. Ever. Not even in the little time I have left. I *should* ask permission every time I kiss her. Because for once I can almost imagine what it feels like to stand in her sandals. (Almost.)

A person should never, ever feel obligated to agree to anything until he or she truly is ready. Period.

Failed with a Capital F

But when the stage lights explode in my face, and the audience responds with a fevered scream, and the band unites on the downbeat—somehow I'm right there: guitar number two. I'm *on it,* note for note. I can't miss; I know "Kosher Firth Day" too well. I've played along to the CD dozens of times. Hundreds. And right then I see that it's true, that all the stupid MTV and VH1 interviews are dead-on: there is nothing like the blast of adrenaline you experience when you first lock into a tight groove, *live,* with sick musicians (your heroes!)—and a crowd of strangers is loving you for it. The energy feeds you, and it feeds *them,* and it grows; the reciprocity makes you mighty, invincible . . . a list of a thousand adjectives couldn't come close to describing it.

And I'm pulling it off.

I've been transformed.

It's not just that I've miraculously overcome any fears and neuroses, that I've conquered the swirling vortex. It's not just that this is a historic moment for *me.* This is a historic moment for *them.* For Shakes the Clown. They've never invited another musician to play with them live before. I'm the first. I know this

DANIEL EHRENHAFT

for a fact. I've downloaded every concert bootleg available. I've downloaded the set lists. I know their history probably better than they do. Which means . . . what, exactly? They're cruel and twisted; they're impulsive; they don't give a crap about anyone but themselves . . . except that little ritual they performed back-stage. . . . Does that mean . . . ?

Am I in Shakes the Clown? For the next nineteen hours, at least? Is my new name Shake 'n Bake?

"Burger!"

The voice is tiny. It sounds like Mark.

"Burger!"

At first I think I'm imagining it. The monitors are deafening. I can hear every drum fill in my teeth and rib cage—but no, that's definitely him. I squint out into the mass of writhing bodies. My eyes still haven't quite adjusted to the glare.

"Burger, your fly's unzipped!"

There. He's mashed up against the edge of the stage, directly opposite Wes—one hand cupped around his face, the other slamming down in time to the music, blissful. He isn't cringing this time. He's smiling. *"Made you look!"* he mouths. I shake my head and smirk back dizzily. Until I spotted him, I hadn't realized how high the stage was. Wes could kick Mark if he stepped out past his microphone stand. (Come to think of it, Wes *would* kick Mark.) And—*Jesus*, there's Nikki! Right next to him! Rachel is there, too, next to *her*, looking not so blissful . . .

and so are Lou and Frankie—*My God*, they're all in a row . . . all right up front . . . packed tightly. . . . I hope none of them get hurt. . . .

I stop smiling.

Suddenly the adrenaline rush fades. Suddenly the vortex starts to swirl again.

I don't get it. I mean, from an objective point of view, everything is perfect. Everything. For Christ's sake: I'm living out an impossible fantasy I've had more times than I'll ever admit! How many people get to do that? Nobody! I'm the luckiest guy in the world! AND my girlfriend and best friend are front and center! This isn't just a fantasy come true; this is a Hallmark moment.

But I can't enjoy it. Because it's bogus. It's all a lie.

First off:

When I discovered Shakes the Clown, I felt as if I were delving into a tiny, special, secret society. But now there are no secrets. Now I know these guys. They won't sell out (even though they should); they don't suck live (not with a second guitarist, anyway); they *are* depraved. Or are they? Or is their depravity just a little forced? They aren't particularly funny—at least, not in the smart-stupid way I imagined them to be. There's no grand scheme, no ironic unifying philosophy behind their dumb jokes. Even though they've technically met every single one of my obsessed-fan/music-geek requirements, they've Failed me. Failed, with a capital *F*. They don't embody Purity. They embody nothing. They *aren't* my heroes.

Second:

The only reason I'm even up here with them is because I didn't have the guts to be honest with Rachel. I ran away from her in the most cowardly way possible. And then as luck would have it, I bumped into Mark, and then I bumped into Nikki, and yada, yada, yada. It was a random series of pie-in-the-face events that saved me. That's all. I had nothing to do with it. No, if I'd had the courage to do what needed to be done, I would still be outside talking to Rachel. But instead I'm onstage in a clown nose—

Oh, crap.

Twig. He's right behind Nikki. He's . . .

Is he fondling her?

He's got his hands on her hips.

She tries to swat them away. He won't let her. This is bad. Very bad. Why did she ever flirt with him at all? Oh, yeah, right: for ME—so she could introduce me to my "heroes" because I would never be motivated enough to meet them on my own.

I scowl at Mark. He grins back at me, giving me a thumbs-up. *No, no, no—I'm not scowling at you because I'm pretending to be tough and mean, like a rock star! Don't look at me! Look at your girlfriend! . . .* But thank God, the others start to notice that there's something wrong. First Rachel. Then Lou and Frankie. They twist toward Nikki, watching uncomfortably. They can't do much about it; it's too crowded. . . . Nikki attempts to squirm free again. Nope. Twig won't let go.

Well. I think I've seen just about enough. I think I'm done blowing stuff off, too. I think I'm ready to take a cue from what Mark did to Leo.

Yes. It's time to start living. It's time to move out of the realm of "should." It's time to act on my anger.

So I unplug the guitar, I march to the edge of the stage, and I kick Twig in the face—as hard as I possibly can.

Now Get on Your Knees, Bend Over, and Thank Me

Five details surrounding the kick:

1. When I unplug Wes's guitar, the speakers emit an excruciating shriek: *EEEEEEEEEE!!!* This retriggers the tinnitus.

2. When my right foot makes contact with Twig's face (or his chins, really; he has several of them), my left foot slides out from under me. I fall hard on my butt in classic, third-rate, Borscht Belt clown style.

3. Since the attack was unexpected, however—since I had the element of surprise on my side and was a regular Angel of Kicking in the Face—I achieve the desired goal. Twig topples away from Nikki with a grunt, "Oof!"

4. Unfortunately, this sets off a chain reaction/domino effect of people falling backward over each other throughout the club.

5. Shakes the Clown continues to play the chorus of "Kosher Firth Day." Its lyrics go:

    You can't teach me to drive, so don't bother
    Or I'll put on some stale old slacks like your father,
    Which means it's time for a spanking,
    Now get on your knees, bend over, and thank me.

Belly Flop

I try to ignore the havoc I've wrought. In the midst of it all I try to ignore the music, the angry yelps from the audience, the shocked expressions of Rachel, Mark, and Nikki (whose face I just barely missed with my toe) . . . and Wes, too, who is in a strategic position to smash his guitar over me or worse. I doubt he'll try anything, though. I have a shield. His prized custom purple banjo-shaped guitar is still strapped around my shoulders. He wouldn't hurt *that*. Although he did toss a practice amplifier into a bucket of beer . . .

I scramble to my feet. "Nikki, come on!"

She gapes at me. "What?"

"Come on! Up here!" I seize her wrists and tug her up

onstage. *Oops.* Bad idea. She's heavier than she looks. I wince. My arms burn. Finally she belly flops at my feet. Success! I hear Wes chuckling ominously into the microphone: *"Mu-hu-ha-ha!"* He stops playing, but Glenda and Herbert still doggedly plug along. The noise reverberates through the club, a crazed goulash of bass and drums. I whirl in place, untangling myself from the strap, shoving the guitar at Wes, hauling Nikki up beside me—

"Ted Burger, you're a true clown," Wes remarks.

I don't answer. I grab Nikki's hand and run. I'm afraid of what else I might do if I stick around any longer.

Not a Jovial, Retirement-Age Italian or Israeli Guy

"Whoa, wait, Ted! Where are we going?"

"Out," I say. My voice sounds strangely nasal. Then I remember: I'm wearing a clown nose. I plunge back down the staircase into the dark maze of corridors, tugging her along behind me as best I can.

She wrenches free of my grip. "Out where?"

"Outside. Away. Far." I skid to a halt in a long, familiar-looking hall. My sneakers screech on the concrete. My head jerks right—*yes!* There's the AUTHORIZED PERSONNEL ONLY sign. Which means the exit is to the left . . . that big door shrouded in darkness at the opposite end. . . . I bolt for it. "Come on."

DANiEL EHRENHAFT

"Ted, wait—"

"Now, Nikki!" I run, grimacing over my shoulder. "We can talk later, okay? But right now a very large bouncer has got it in for me. Understand?"

"I . . ." She shakes her head but follows.

I tear off the clown nose as I burst through the door. The awful streetlamp bears down on me. *Crap.* I freeze. I'm back in the yard again—the huge, maximum-security prison yard that is the Bronx.

Nikki shuts the door behind us.

A stroke of temporary luck: the sidewalk is deserted. Nobody has managed to chase us. Not yet. It might have been wise to come up with a plan before I kicked a four-ton bouncer in the face. Oh, well. We can hide in a bodega or—

Wait a second.

There's a big black Lincoln Town Car idling across the street. A cardboard sign is propped up in the driver's side window:

TRIBECA LIMO 410

"Rachel, I love you," I whisper out loud.

Nikki stares at me. "What did you just say?"

"I'll explain later." I grab her hand again and dash to the car—throwing the back door open and tossing her inside as if she were a piece of luggage—then tumble in after her. The seats are plush and velvety. The air is cool and quiet. *Safety*, I think. "Uh, hi," I mutter at the driver as I fumble with the door lock.

"Are you Burger?"

The voice is female, heavily accented . . . almost musical. Caribbean, maybe? I squint up at the front seat. The driver is a slender, attractive black woman. She looks to be in her midthirties. I'm surprised. Every single time I've taken Tribeca Limos in the past, the driver has been a jovial, retirement-age Italian or Israeli guy.

"Yes," I say.

"Barrow Street?" she asks, pulling away from the curb.

I glance out the window. Twig and several murderous-looking hoodlums have emerged from the front door.

"Ted?" Nikki prompts nervously. "Barrow Street?"

"No. We're going to JFK."

Appetizer

Only after the Town Car has safely zipped onto the Cross Bronx Expressway—far from the intersection of Brooks Avenue and 151st Street—does Nikki finally clear her throat and speak up.

"Ted? I know you said we had to go outside and away and far, but don't you think the airport is pushing it?"

"Give me the list," I say.

She lifts an eyebrow. "What?"

DANIEL EHRENHAFT

"The list. You know, the *list*."

"You mean the napkin?"

"Yes." I nod. I don't trust myself to talk much beyond that. Because I'm barely able to contain myself. *I might start break-ing into the funky chicken.* Ever since we sped away from the Onyx, I've been overcome with a giddy euphoria. It ripples through my body in wave after wave. I forget the poison. I for-get being mean to Rachel. And I thought that playing onstage with Shakes the Clown was a rush? Or that anger alone could quash tinnitus and nausea? Ha! The *real* rush, the *real* salve comes when you finally prove—

"Ted, what happened back there?"

"Huh?"

"What the hell were you thinking? You could have gotten yourself killed, you know that?"

I shrug. "Yeah, I know. I just—I saw that Twig was putting his hands all over you, and . . . I don't know." I shift in the seat, too twitchy to keep still. "Now can you hand over the list?"

She looks at me the way a psychiatrist would look at a long-term patient who can't make progress. *I'm sorry; the therapy has failed. You require institutionalization.*

"What?" I demand.

"Nothing, Ted. Nothing. But this conversation isn't over."

"I never said it was."

With a sigh she pulls the napkin from her pocket. It's so wet and crumpled that it's close to disintegrating.

I catch a whiff of Budweiser as I unfold it. To me, it smells like triumph. I take a moment to breathe evenly, to calm down a little.

BURGER'S SPRING BREAK

1. Lose virginity.
2. Jam with Shakes the Clown.
3. *PARTY* with Shakes the Clown.
4. Get back at Billy Rifkin.
5. Do something truly heroic. Like rescue a baby from a burning building.
6. Along these lines, actually *GO* to one of those third world countries Rachel is always talking about and do something positive *THERE*. (Like Nigeria or wherever. But fast.)
7. Rob a bank.
8. Pull a crazy stunt, like bungee jump off the GW Bridge.
9. Start your own religion.
10. Get something named after you (like a park or a fountain).

The words have been blurred with brown liquid and hours of abuse, but they're still legible. I smile to myself as I reexamine the ten tasks. My mission is just getting started. Amen! With that single kick, I've tasted life. I've had an appetizer. Now it's time for the main course. And I've got the next eighteen hours to gorge myself on it.

Another Big, Huge Favor

"So, Ted?" Nikki says.

"Yeah?" I say, my eyes roving over the list.

"Can you please tell me why you kicked that guy in the face and why we ran away from everyone? Not that I mind. I'm just curious. That's all."

Ran away?

I blink and look up. I guess I did run away. But that part of my life is over. Without a doubt.

"Well, it's like this," I tell her. "And I'm not joking, so don't laugh."

"I'm not really in a laughing mood," she says wryly.

I smile. For a second I find myself staring back at her in that dim, hallucinatory, speeding-cab light. *How does she do it?* I wonder. *How does she manage to appear so relaxed, as if this is all just part of a normal night?* It's making *me* relaxed. Which I know is intentional. But with her black jean jacket hanging off one shoulder, and her black hair a mess, and those benevolent alien eyes—

Hmmm. I really need to stop that: the thinking-too-much-about-Nikki's-appearance thing. That part of my life is over, too.

"It all comes back to the clown thing," I say, trying to focus. "I was up there with that clown nose on my face. I was up onstage, knowing I've always been a clown, with a clown band, and . . ." I pause. "I figured I had to be more like Mark for once, you know?"

The eyes bore into my own. "Like Mark?" she repeats.

"Yeah. Like the kind of guy who dives in and saves the day. It's just . . . Mark has this incredible faith that something amazing is always just around the bend. And because he believes it, it's true. Mark *makes* amazing stuff happen. He tackled Leo to the ground! He affects the world! But I'm the opposite. The world affects *me*. So I wanted to change it up. Besides, you were being molested."

Nikki doesn't respond. She smiles sadly.

"What?"

"Nothing," she says.

"Listen, Nikki, can you do me a really huge favor?"

"Of course." She straightens and leans close. A few strands of black hair fall in her eyes. Reflexively I brush them out of the way so we can see each other.

"Can you promise me that we won't talk about the past anymore? I mean, this is my night. Like you said? Not to sound ungrateful . . . the Shakes the Clown thing blew me away—but can you promise me that we'll only talk about the list?"

She nods, looking down at her lap.

"Anything you want," she whispers.

No Baggage

I spread out the napkin in front of her. My hands are shaking—more than they've shaken since I've been poisoned. I'm not sure why. Probably not a good idea to dwell on it. Nikki doesn't notice, or she pretends not to.

"See, the way I figure it, I've already taken care of five and a half of these things."

She laughs. "Five and a half?"

"Yeah. I mean, not exactly. But just look. Skip number one, obviously. Number two: I jammed with Shakes the Clown. And they poured beer over my head, so that counts as partying, right? Number three. Okay, number four's a tough one. I didn't get *back* at Billy Rifkin. I got *with* Billy Rifkin. So that's a yes. Number five: No, I didn't rescue a baby from a burning building, but I got Twig's hands off you. So that's another yes. And the way I see it, kicking Twig in the face counts for seven and eight as well." I glance up at her, satisfied. "Five and a half. See?"

"Sure. But tell me, Ted. How does kicking Twig in the face count for robbing a bank or bungee jumping off a bridge?"

"It's the *spirit* of the thing," I explain. "It all comes back to what you said at the diner. It's about embracing the Dark Side. Wouldn't you say that kicking a guy in the face counts as embracing the Dark Side? Even more than robbing a bank? Because, you know, theoretically, nobody would get hurt in a bank robbery. So painwise it's a victimless crime. Kicking is much worse. And similarly, kicking a guy who's ten zillion times your size—*and* who's a sex fiend with a penchant for dismantling people to boot—is a hell of a lot more dangerous than bungee jumping off the GW Bridge, right?"

Whew. Talk about diarrhea of the mouth. I haven't run my mouth this hard or this fast since that fateful day I first explained to Rachel about why I loved Shakes the Clown.

Nikki smirks. "Oh, I get it," she says teasingly, in the sort of deadpan voice that late-night talk show hosts use to silence dumb hecklers. "As long as you kicked a guy in the face, you've lived. Gee, Ted. You make a very strong case. I apologize."

"Ha, ha," I tease back, in the same deadpan voice.

She lays her ringed fingers on my knee—just for an instant. "So you never answered my question," she says.

"Yes, I did! I told you why I assaulted Twig!"

"No, the other question. Why are we going to JFK?"

I point at the napkin. "Because, as you've suggested, I *haven't* lived yet. See for yourself. I have to go to Nigeria. But don't worry. You aren't coming with me. Well, not unless you

DANiEL EHRENHAFT

want to. Do you want to? Just kidding. I'll have the driver take you home. Which, by the way, is another instance of robbery because Rachel's parents are paying for this whole entire ride—"

"Nigeria?" the cabdriver interrupts. "Did you say you were going to Nigeria?"

"Yes? Why?"

She smiles at me in the rearview mirror. "I have an uncle who lives in Lagos. I'm from Sierra Leone."

"Oh." I smile back. I'm not sure what I'm supposed to say.

"The reason I ask is because you have no baggage," she adds. "How long will you be staying in Nigeria?"

Nikki buries her face in her hands. I can't tell if she's sad or embarrassed. Maybe both. *Why did I just invite her to come with me?*

The driver laughs. She obviously doesn't believe that I intend to fly to Africa tonight. For some reason, I find this extremely annoying.

"Another reason I ask: Do you have a passport?" she says.

"Yeah, I do," I answer.

I yank my passport out of my back pocket and flap it in the air for her to see. It's a little the worse for wear—having been stuffed into various pairs of pants for the past year—but it's *valid,* and I'm sure it will get me on a flight. So why is she giving me a hard time? I'm utterly wholehearted about this. I *am* going to Nigeria. As sure as I kicked Twig in the face. As sure as

I'll start a religion about a doughnut-shaped universe. The clock is ticking, and I've been galvanized.

"Do you mind if I ask you something else?" the woman says.

"Not at all," I lie.

"What is the purpose of your visit?"

Good question. Excellent question.

I should answer it before that giddy euphoria slips away. I should be candid about my feelings. I should let loose in that honest, intimate way that you can only with perfect strangers—with that freedom you get when you know you'll never see a person again. I have nothing to worry about. I can confess whatever I want to this woman, without any repercussions. I'll be dead by this time tomorrow. And in answering her, I'll have answered my *own* questions. I'll have further liberated *myself*. Besides, Nikki deserves to hear this, too.

"You want to know why?" I answer. "Because I'm dying. I don't have a whole lot of time, and I've always lived a sheltered and lazy life. I want to see how the rest of the world lives, just for a brief moment. Because if I go someplace where there is real sickness and poverty and crimes against humanity and if I can *help* in some way—if I can do just one little thing, once, I don't know. I'll feel good. Because for the first time ever—tonight, just now—I *felt* something. And I want to hold on to that feeling. I want to milk it for all it's worth. Okay?"

The woman bursts out laughing.

Nice. Well. That went over perfectly. I'm glad I could entertain. My sense of comic timing isn't as lousy as I believed.

"Only a child would say something like that!" she cries.

You can stop now, please. I slump down into the car seat. At least it's dark in here. Wouldn't it be great if I could die right this second and just get it over with? Nikki touches my knee again, very briefly. I'm not sure what the gesture means, but I can't bring myself to look at her. I don't think I'll *ever* be able to look at her. No, I have a feeling this current bout of embarrassment will last me a long, long time—as in forever.

"I don't mean any disrespect," the woman adds apologetically. "I just mean that perhaps you should spend the time you have left with your girlfriend. You know, instead of running away? She's beautiful!" She beams at Nikki in the mirror. "But you certainly don't need to travel the world to do good things. The world is an ugly place. Every city is the same. Lagos is no different than New York. Both have McDonald's. Both have suffering. There is only one difference between America and the rest of the world: people outside America know what it is like to live with death. They see death around them all the time. But people in America believe that they are going to live forever. Perhaps that is why you are running. You are afraid of death. But no matter how fast and far you run, even to Nigeria, you are not going to outrun death."

I open my mouth to answer, to argue—and then stop.

What's the point? I saw what opening my big mouth did for me the last time: it bought me a one-way ticket to the Land of Humiliation. But that's all right; I'm used to it there. I've lived there most of my (short!) life. Sure, I vacationed for a while back at the Onyx, but now I'm back where I belong. The prodigal son has returned.

Except, Madam Cabdriver, you *are* wrong about one thing: I'm not trying to outrun death. I'm just trying to run, period—to move, to go places, to do things instead of sitting on my butt during my last hours. Is that so bad? And so what if I'm afraid? Who isn't afraid of dying? Name one person! And for God's sake, lady, did you have to insinuate that Nikki was my girlfriend? Thanks a lot! Way to make things awkward!

You're wrong about something else, too.

I have plenty of baggage. You just can't see it. It's swirling around with the guilt and the poison and all the rest of the crap I've got stowed up there.

Fingers

The three of us exchange very few words for the rest of the drive. I wonder what Nikki is thinking. I know what *I'm* thinking. I'm thinking about how she was right: I ran away. Again. I left Mark and Rachel back at the Onyx. I'm thinking about what

Twig will do to them if he finds them, especially if he discovers that they're my best friend and my girlfriend.

"Nikki, you don't have a cell phone, do you?" I finally ask when the JFK exit signs start appearing with alarming frequency. "I left mine at home."

She shakes her head. "I left mine at home, too."

I lean forward. "Excuse me, ma'am?" I ask the driver. "You wouldn't happen to have a cell phone, would you?"

"Yes, I do," she replies. "But it's not for you. I have to keep the line open."

"Oh. Right. Of course." I smile. I'm tempted to lunge forward and strangle her, but I don't—mostly because Nikki might die, too, if the car goes out of control. I collapse into the cushions. Flat marshlands whiz past the window. I hear the roar of a descending plane. We're very close.

"Who do you want to call, Ted?" Nikki asks.

"I want to call Mark or Rachel," I mumble. "I want to see if they got out okay."

"Oh," Nikki says.

She takes my hand. She squeezes it between both of hers.

I turn toward her—clumsily, a little taken aback by the physical contact. It's odd: she's held my hand before (dragging me various places), but I sense right away that this is different. This isn't nannyish or maternal. . . . Actually, I don't know what it is.

And defying logic, it makes me feel terrible. It makes me feel *more* angry and embarrassed and ashamed.

"You're something else, you know that?" she whispers.

"Yeah, you told me that once."

She stares at our jumble of intertwined fingers. A melancholy smile spreads across her face. "Can I ask you one thing?"

I swallow. "Of course."

"When you were onstage tonight—you know, at first, right when you started to play—you were super-psyched, weren't you?"

"Yeah. I guess."

"But then you weren't. Something changed."

"Well, yeah, I saw that Twig was coming up behind you."

She shakes her head. "No, even before that. I was watching you. In the middle of the song . . . You looked down at us, and you looked at the band—and then it was like, a light in your eyes went out. You looked really depressed."

I stare at her, amazed. "You *saw* that?"

"It wasn't hard to see. But the thing is, I think I know what you were thinking, maybe. And this is just a guess: but were you bummed that Shakes the Clown didn't live up your expectations? I mean, were you thinking—*Oh, man, this is great; this is just what I always dreamed of; this is gonna become part of the whole Shakes the Clown history, and lore, and legend—and I'm in it . . . but still, somehow, it just doesn't cut it?*"

I'm stunned.

No, *stunned* isn't strong enough a word. *Nikki just read my mind.* That's no exaggeration. She articulated everything I wanted to but couldn't before, not concisely, anyway; she articulated exactly what was going on—inside *me.* It's scary. It's terrifying. It's exhilarating, too, though, I have to say. Nobody's ever understood me like that. Nobody's ever even come close to being in the same ballpark . . . the same galaxy. I try to answer, but the words get stuck in my throat.

"The thing is," she continues, "I know it's not exactly the same situation—but sometimes that's how I feel with Mark. I mean, I expect him to be one thing, but he isn't. He doesn't measure up. Like tonight! He hired a prostitute. I mean, I know why he did it, and it was funny on one level . . . but on another it was really, really uncool. And I told him so. I knew you'd agree. But did he listen? No. He didn't even notice what *you* noticed from the stage, that Twig or whatever the hell his name is was grabbing me. *He* should have done something. Not you."

I shake my head. "But . . . but—he was watching me perform," I stammer thickly. "He didn't even see it."

"Well, that's the whole point, isn't it?"

"What is?"

"That our relationship isn't what it's cracked up to be," she murmurs. "On the outside, everything looks perfect. It's almost like we have to *make* it look perfect because we've been going out for so long. Because people expect it. Most of all, because *you* expect it. Sometimes we act like these parodies of ourselves just for your benefit. It's not even conscious." She lets out a deep breath. "You know what, Ted? Mark and I depend on you a lot more than you probably know. A lot more."

Wow.

That's . . . well, that's heavy. I don't know what to say or even if I'm supposed to say anything. So I don't. I try to be like Nikki for once. I try not to run my mouth. I try to let my silence speak for me. I keep gazing at our hands, for lack of anything better to do. And then a puzzling thing happens: one of her fingers caresses mine. Very delicately. Nothing more than a brush. I can't even tell if it's deliberate or not. Was it just a tic, an involuntary flutter?

I shouldn't think about it, though. No. Bad to go there. I should think about something else, like how fascinated I am by how *cold* her fingers are. They're as cold as her rings. It's as if there's no difference between them.

She shivers, glancing up at me. Her face drifts toward mine. I see nothing but those eyes. They're two shiny black asteroids floating in the vastness of space—and due to chance or astrophysics or both, they've drifted too close to my own . . . right into their gravitational fields. We're caught now. No force in the universe can prevent us from changing course. The attraction is too strong. It's irreversible.

I've been waiting for this all my life. And now my life is about to end.

Involuntarily I pounce, Rachel style.

Nikki pounces back.

The speed and ferocity are almost scary. I feel a blast of euphoria, the same swift kick to the central nervous system I got when the lights came up onstage at the Onyx. In an instant our lips are mashed together, and we're clawing at each other and stroking each other's hair—

This was no accident. This is destiny.

Betrayal

"Sorry to break this up, but what airline?" the driver demands.

Nikki and I spring apart.

Holy—What did I just do? Poof! The euphoria vaporizes. The sense of destiny follows. Now I'm frightened and hyperventilating. Bad. Wrong. Betrayal. Dark Side. I shouldn't have gone there. So why did I? Why? And . . . *Oh, boy,* and now the tinnitus, the nausea, the vertigo—yes, the whole Poison Crew has returned, bursting in on me like a bunch of old pals at a surprise party: *We're ba-a-ack! Betcha weren't expecting us!* I clutch at the door handle. *Jesus.* We've already arrived at the international departure gates: a morass of traffic and pedestrians and luggage and security and lighted signs, EL AL, AIR INDIA, VIRGIN ATLANTIC, NIGERIA AIRWAYS—

"What airline?" the woman repeats impatiently.

"Wherever you can pull over," I choke out. I glance at Nikki in wide-eyed horror.

"I think I should go home," she says.

"Right." The response is instant. She isn't coming with me. No surprise there. I can't read her voice, either, but it doesn't matter. Nothing matters. *Must escape. Now.*

She bites her lip. "Ted, I—"

"Don't worry about it. I'll pay Rachel back for the fare. Just tell the driver where you want to go."

Nikki's face falls. "That wasn't what I meant. Ted, you need to come with me so we can get you to a hospital. We have to stop playing this stupid game—"

"Good night!" I say, with deranged cheer. I leap out of the car before it comes to a complete stop. I don't bother closing the door, either; I simply careen across the pavement toward the nearest entrance, doubled over and gagging. Several pedestrians pause to observe me. They appear understandably disturbed.

Sometimes it helps to be a sniveling coward.

Other times it doesn't.

Sleep on the Red-Eye

I don't expect to get very far. I expect to start vomiting very soon after I barrel through the revolving doors at Terminal E. Especially since the light inside is of the same fluorescent prison-yard variety that blinded me on the sidewalk outside the Onyx. The air in here is frigid, too. It's even colder than the lobby at Billy Rifkin's. And the smooth granite tile is . . . swimming toward my face?

I straighten up. I shake off the tinnitus and vertigo and nausea. I summon my will. And within a matter of seconds, with a concentrated effort, I'm functioning well enough to purchase a ticket. I whirl in place, searching for a clock. There are dozens of computer monitors, and people and—*there*. A big round clock, above the DEPARTURE GATES sign. 10:15. Perfect. I'll catch the red-eye to Lagos and sleep on the flight. Maybe I won't even wake up! I can always hope for the best. Because no matter what happens, I won't be coming home. Not alive, anyway. It'll be impossible.

Right.

Lagos, here I come!

I figure by the time I've landed and cleared customs there, I'll have about one hour to live. Which will be fine. I can already picture it: I'll be the mysterious, solitary American boy—ghostlike, known in certain circles as the Walking Dead. But the

Nigerians won't see my wickedness and degradation. I'll keep it hidden deep inside. I'll have no past. Yet in that final hour, I'll become a legend out on those hot streets, shuttling between one McDonald's and the next, lending a hand to all those who suffer before the poison shuts me down in a blaze of glory. . . . Oh, man! It's gonna be great!

Change of Plan

Another massive stroke of luck: there's no line at the Nigeria Airways ticket counter. Woo-hoo! I march up to a very nice-looking, heavyset black man in a green-and-white uniform.

"Hello!" I greet him.

"Hello!" he replies, matching my inappropriate enthusiasm. His accent is not unlike the cabdriver's. "May I help you?"

"I'd like one ticket to Lagos, please!" I say. "On the next available flight!"

"Certainly! I'll need your passport and visa!"

"My passport and . . . what?"

"Your visa."

"Oh. Right." My enthusiasm fades.

"No visa?"

"Well." I glance over my shoulder, just to make sure a line hasn't formed behind me, and then I lean across the desk. "Let me ask you something," I whisper. "Where can I go in Africa that doesn't require a visa?"

"And why would you want to be flying to someplace that doesn't require a visa?" he asks me politely.

"Because I just want to, all right?" I whisper.

His smile evaporates. "No, young man, that is not all right. We have certain security procedures in place." He doesn't sound so polite anymore; he sounds perturbed. "Please wait here." He picks up a phone, eyeing me cautiously.

Wait here?

Do I really want to do that? No. No, I don't think I do. In fact, I want to be somewhere else, fast, and I know exactly where I can go—not just in terms of this airport, but also in terms of the world. Yes. My parents took me to London when I graduated junior high. And I specifically remember that I didn't need a visa. All I needed was a passport and my school ID—both of which I happen to have on me right now. And we flew Virgin Atlantic, in this very terminal. So I'm set.

London, here I come!

No Credit

Much to my dismay, there *is* a line at the Virgin Atlantic ticket counter. It's not particularly long, just a couple of people, but it is long enough to give me a few minutes to think. And that is not what I need right now. Since I left Nikki, I've come to the most important conclusion of my (short) life: thought in any form equals unhealthy. *Lazy* people think. *Clowns* think. We doers, however, we *don't* think. We just *do*. Which is why I won't allow myself to wonder about Nikki's feelings, or about the fates of Mark or Rachel, or about Rachel's feelings, or Mark's feelings—

"Next, please!" a cheery British voice calls out.

I'm up.

The woman behind the desk is about my mother's age. She has the most grotesque set of crooked teeth I've ever seen. They're even worse than Phurm Hand Shake's yellow, rodent-like chompers. I try not to look at her mouth.

"Hello!" I say. "I'd like a one-way ticket to London, please?"

She tilts her head. "Will you be traveling alone?"

"Yes. Yes, I will." I fumble for my wallet and passport and slap them down in front of her. "No baggage, either. Just me!"

"I see." She looks me in the eye. "One moment, please."

She lifts her phone and presses a button, then hangs up.

"Is there a problem?" I ask.

"No . . . No problem at all." She flashes a brief, horrific smile before turning to her computer monitor. "Would you like to depart on the next available flight, then?"

I heave a sigh of relief. "Yes. Please."

DANiEL EHRENHAFT

"Well, let's see. . . ." She types rapidly on her keyboard. "Yes, I can get you on the eleven p.m. You'll have to hurry, though. The fare is fourteen hundred dollars."

My eyes bulge. "Fourteen hundred—?" I suck in my breath and muster a smile. "No problem." But as I fish the credit card out of my wallet, I can't keep my hands from shaking again. They're shaking even harder than they were in the cab. Is it the poison, or is it my anxiety? Maybe this isn't such a great idea.

The woman plucks the card from my spastic fingers and swipes it through the magnetic reader. She then places it beside her, out of my reach.

Uh-oh.

The dizziness creeps back up again, like a strong tide, gathering force. The tinnitus rings at a fever pitch: *EEEEEEEEEEEE!!!* My breath comes in short gasps. My stomach doesn't even exist anymore. It feels as if it's been pulverized and discarded, surgically removed with a blunt hatchet. I hold on to the counter to steady myself. I don't think I can stand much longer. I might have to sit on the floor.

"I'm sorry, sir," the woman says. Her voice sounds far away. "Your card has been declined."

"Declined?" I croak.

"Yes. It appears you have no available credit. Not on this card." She smiles once more. Her eyes flicker away from me.

She nods, almost imperceptibly. "Now, if you'd like . . ." She leaves the sentence hanging, staring behind my head.

Is somebody back there?

I whirl around to see three large cops, all of whom are reaching for me—

Black Hole of Nothingness

That's pretty much it.

Honestly, that's all I remember. Passing out is short on detail and long on aftermath, at least for the person who experiences it. The best way to describe it . . . well, it feels as if the swirling vortex somehow manages to bust loose from my skull, like a wild animal escaping the zoo—and then it gobbles me up and swallows me down into a black hole of nothingness.

Only it's not nearly as exciting as that.

Preface to the Great Gig in the Sky

Sometimes, even now, I wonder if states of unconsciousness are like fingerprints, if no two are alike. I guess there are probably patterns, depending on an individual's psyche. Lots of people

DANIEL EHRENHAFT

do share the same sorts of archetypal dreams, after all. So say, for example, that you're a chickenhearted, self-absorbed clown (among other things) and you believe you're going to die. . . . An unconscious state might trigger guilty visions of your own funeral. Yes? Maybe?

This is just a guess.

Death of a Clown: I

SCENE: *Outside our old synagogue on West Thirteenth Street. Pouring rain. A big sign on the little patch of grass:* TED BURGER FUNERAL CANCELED.

My parents hurry up to the rabbi as he's locking the front door.

"Why was our son's funeral canceled?" they ask.

The rabbi shakes his head. "Ted was a coward, Mr. and Mrs. Burger. Nobody particularly cares to mourn the loss of a coward."

They look at each other.

"I guess you're right," Mom agrees. "Besides that, he spent far too much time in his room playing guitar."

Dad shrugs. "Well, then, we probably should be heading back to that billboard convention ay-sap, wouldn't you say?"

Death of a Clown: II

SCENE: *The Rikers Island morgue. My corpse on a concrete slab.*

Nobody will claim the body. My parents disowned me after they discovered that a prostitute ransacked their liquor cabinet. Nikki has long since renounced any friendship with me because I tried to run away to Africa—but then was arrested and hauled away at JFK for suspicious behavior. Rachel has renounced me for the lies.

Finally Mark shows up.

"Yeah, I'm here for Ted Burger," he tells the guards. "I shouldn't be. I heard that right before he died, he tried to scam on my girlfriend. So if I were you, I'd just toss this scumbag in the East River. Maybe the fish will eat him. At least then he'll do some good for once. What goes around comes around. People are dogs, you know?"

Death of a Clown: III

SCENE: *A cemetery. A lone burial plot. My casket, descending into the earth.*

It's the end of the service. Dad steps up to the podium. He pulls a folded letter out of his pocket. "Before we conclude here today, Ted asked that I read something. He wrote it just before the poison consumed him completely. He wanted to honor his friend Mark. It's just a short statement."

He clears his throat: "'Mark was my best friend. We had our ups and downs. But I must say that I never met anybody more honest than Mark. And that's a pretty weird assertion, considering he was an impulsive maniac.

"'Actually, forget that. It makes no sense. All I'm trying to say is that I was lucky to know him. He made me realize that you don't have to do a bunch of crazy stuff to make your life complete. You just have to DEAL with life. You have to hang out with the people you love and not BS them. And if more people were like Mark, I personally think we'd be a lot better off. Then maybe we could start seeing the important stuff.'"

Doubt

The first thing I notice is that I'm lying in bed.

It's a good sign. Generally, in those documentaries about the afterlife, you hear about walking into bright light. You hear about being on your feet. Except . . . wherever I am, the light *is* pretty bright.

"Ted?"

I don't recognize the voice.

"Ted? Can you hear me?"

"Yes?" *Wow.* I don't recognize my voice, either. My throat is bone dry. I sound like one of those old guys who hang out at the Off-Track Betting near our school.

"How do you feel?" the voice asks.

I'm not sure. I don't even know if I'm still alive. It's a man's voice—but maybe not so deep and ponderous that it could belong to a divine entity. I hope not, anyway.

"I don't know," I croak. "Pretty confused, I guess."

"Do you know where you are?"

"No."

"You're at St. Mary's Hospital in Brooklyn, Ted. You had a panic attack."

Brooklyn? I force myself to open my eyes all the way, blinking rapidly to clear the glare. A fuzzy face floats directly above me, framed by several lights. Gradually the face grows clearer. . . . He's bearded, ruddy, with glasses, in his late thirties or early forties. . . . He's wearing a white coat. He's holding a clipboard.

"You gave us all quite a scare," he says. "For a lot of different reasons."

I shake my head, struggling to sit up straight. "I . . . I . . ."

"Hold on!" he cajoles. He lays a hand on my shoulder, easing me back down into the pillow. "Just relax. The sedative will

     DANIEL EHRENHAFT

take a while to wear off. But I do have some good news for you, Ted. You weren't poisoned."

Once again I try to prop myself up on my elbows. It's no use. I'm becoming aware of other details, though. My clothes are gone. I've been dressed in a hospital gown. Something is sticking into my arm, too, an IV of some kind. It stings. Clear liquid drips into it from a plastic Baggie suspended on the bedpost. There's also an annoying *beep beep beep*.

"We gave you an anesthetic earlier," the doctor says. "That's why you're just waking up now. Nothing major; we wanted to run some tests. Your friend's father notified us." He glances at the clipboard. "Joshua Singer, an administrator at St. Vincent's? He contacted us immediately upon your friend's request. He advised us of this incident at the diner in Manhattan, so we felt it prudent to rule a few things out as soon as possible. As I said, the good news is that—"

"Wait, wait," I interrupt. "I'm sorry. How did I *get* here?"

"Your friend took care of it."

My friend?

His eyes fall to the clipboard again. "Yes. Mark Singer. He found you at the airport. Apparently he explained to the police what was going on. You'll probably have to give a statement at some point, but we can talk about that later."

A statement?

It's hopeless. The more this guy talks, the more baffled I become. I guess I should be glad that *Mark* knows what's going on. I sure as hell don't.

"He can explain it to you better than I can," the doctor says. "Would you like to see him? He's waiting outside."

I nod, very vigorously.

"I'll send him in."

He extends a hand. I shake it, on autopilot.

"My name is Dr. Webb, by the way," he adds. "And just so you know, your parents will be here soon. They're on a flight from Denver right now."

"I . . . okay." *Mom and Dad are coming.* I'm not quite sure how to feel about this news. I'll have a lot of explaining to do. Which will be difficult.

"I'll be back in a little while to check up on you and answer any questions you might have," Dr. Webb says on his way out the door. "Okay?"

"Okay, thanks," I call after him.

Somehow I have a feeling that even if Dr. Webb gave me twenty-four straight hours of his time, he couldn't *possibly* answer all the questions I might have. But I should probably give him the benefit of the doubt. Doubt is pretty much all I have to hold on to right now.

Caveman Style

"Ted!" Mark exclaims.

"Ted? Did you just call me—?"

"Yeah." He pulls up a chair and sits beside me. "I called you Ted."

He looks terrible, exhausted. His hair is even messier than usual. He's also wearing a plain white T-shirt. This is unsettling because it indicates that a fairly significant amount of time has passed since I last saw him. I have no idea if it's day or night, come to think of it. There are no windows in here.

"You've never called me Ted," I gasp hoarsely.

"Yeah, well, Burger died, dude," he says.

"What?"

Mark leans back. The chair squeaks on the linoleum.

"Didn't you hear?" he says. "*Burger* was poisoned. He went out strong, though. He played with his favorite band, and kicked a guy in the head, and then he went to the airport and tried to steal away with his best friend's girlfriend—and he keeled over, right before the cops could get him. But he's gone now. Long gone."

I stare at him, speechless.

"You want to hear something funny about Burger's final, glorious day, though?" he whispers. He leans forward and glances toward the open door. "See, his best friend hired this escort named Joy. And it probably wasn't such a great idea. Because she snagged one of the receipts that fell out of the drawer—you know, when his best friend was looking for his parents' Polaroid? And she stole the credit card number and maxed it out. You see where I'm going with this?"

I shake my head, uncomprehending.

"I'm sure you will," Mark says. "Just give it some time to sink in."

"But . . . airport . . . cops . . . how . . . what . . . ?" I can't do much more than produce monosyllabic grunts, caveman style.

"See, after Burger ran out of the club, his best friend managed to slip out with his girlfriend and her two meathead brothers," Mark says.

I nod, still just as lost.

"Forget it." He drops the silly tone. "Here's what happened. Rachel told me that she'd ordered a car service for you. And when she and I found out you *took* it, we found out you went to Terminal E at JFK. So I thought that you'd lost your mind and decided to take this list seriously. The last part, at least." He pulls the napkin from his pocket and waves it front of me. "You know, *this*? So I chased you down at the airport. And when I got there . . . oh, man." He shakes his head and laughs, running his other hand through his hair. "Well, I was lucky I found you when I did because you were lying on the floor, surrounded by cops. They thought you were dangerous. You were all disheveled, and you stank of beer, and you insisted on getting on an international flight."

"I stank of beer?"

Mark raises his eyebrows. "The doctor said your hair was soaked with it."

Oh, right. I'd almost forgotten about Herbert's baptism.

"So anyway. Look, you want this?" He lays the napkin on my nightstand.

I barely notice. I'm gazing at him, fighting to understand. "What was the deal with Leo?" I ask. "I thought I was—"

"He *lied*," Mark interrupts, lowering his voice and leaning close again. "It was all a lie. He got all that crap about blowfish off the Internet. He tried to scare us. He made it all up! He was a chemistry student, but he flunked out. He's a couple of chairs short of a dining room set, you know what I'm saying? Personally, I don't think he should be tried as a criminal. I think he's insane. He shouldn't be held responsible for his actions."

I agree. I'm not even mad at Leo. He isn't the only one who shouldn't be held responsible for his actions. I hope not, anyway. He just flipped out. He'd reached the end of his rope. Lord knows I can relate. Poison or not, I *was* sick. Leo may be insane, but I'm running a close second. I might have even taken the lead. My actions were a lot worse. Like the Nikki thing, for one . . .

"But look, I think you should keep the napkin," Mark says. "It'll be a memento. You can frame it and put it up with all those pictures on your wall. Hey, that reminds me!" He reaches into his other pocket and pulls out a wrinkled Polaroid. "You definitely should have *this*. If anything belongs on your wall, *this* does. I mean, just look at it. Joy may be running around with your credit card number, but she does take a nice picture."

I manage a faint smile. It's the photo of Mark, diving across my lap in the living room, right before I ran downstairs to hop in a cab with Nikki. Mark is posing—his eyes and mouth are wide open. His tongue is sticking out. I'm wincing. It's an action shot, but we look strangely fake, the way people always do in Polaroids.

Mark pats my shoulder and hands it to me. "Enjoy it. I'm just gonna run downstairs and say good-bye to my dad. He's gotta go to work." He stands and heads for the door.

"Wait, Mark!"

"Yeah?"

"What day is it?"

"What day? It's the first day of the rest of your life!" He winks. "Just kidding. I got that from a sign downstairs in the ER."

Pieces of the Puzzle

Over the course of the next hour or so, I fill in some blanks. Or I suppose I do. Lying there alone in that room, waiting for Dr. Webb, or Mark, or *anybody* . . . I don't have much else to occupy my time. It seems clear that I collapsed at the airport and that

Mark somehow convinced the cops to let me go—or at least to take me to a hospital. It also seems clear that I'm in major, major trouble. Or I will be. Because if what Mark said about Joy is true, then my parents are going to find out about it. And naturally, they'll want to know: How did a hooker/felon ever get in a position to steal my credit card number in the first place?

Which will lead to a lot of other unpleasant questions. Like, where is all their booze?

Probably best to worry about that later. At least, not until Mom and Dad show up. I don't want to suffer another panic attack.

A few big pieces of the puzzle are still missing, though. Namely, Rachel and Nikki. Do they know I'm here? And if they do, did Nikki tell Mark what happened?

Meaning, does he know . . . about the end of the cab ride? But of course he's talked to Nikki. He must have *seen* Nikki; otherwise he wouldn't have had the napkin. *She* had it the last time I was conscious. So she gave it to him. Which means . . . *what?*

Come to think of it, I should worry about all this later, too. This is a puzzle I don't really feel like solving.

Venting

When Dr. Webb reappears, his face is buried in a folder.

"How are you feeling, Ted?" he asks, full of gusto.

I shrug under my blanket. "Okay, I guess. Thirsty."

"Yes, you were very dehydrated! We're taking care of that intravenously." He snaps the folder shut and smiles, adjusting his glasses. "So. Any questions?"

"Yeah. What's a panic attack?"

"Ah, yes! Very good question!" He sits down in Mark's chair. "First of all, just to reassure you, it can't kill you. It's fairly common, in fact. And it's treatable. So you aren't dying. I just want to make that perfectly clear. Do you understand? You aren't dying. You haven't been poisoned."

I nod, feeling vaguely cowed. I didn't want to die. I just thought I was going to.

"What happens is . . ." He sighs. "Well, let me explain it this way. Everybody experiences stress. The healthy way to deal with stress is to talk about it, to confront it. Otherwise it just builds and builds inside you. Are you following me so far?"

"Yeah. The more you keep things inside you, the sicker you feel."

He laughs. "Exactly! But you see, Ted, I'm concerned that you've kept too much inside for a very long time. This is precisely why you acted the way you did. When you thought you were sick, you decided to go off on this crazy adventure instead of dealing with it. And that's why we feel that counseling will—"

DANIEL EHRENHAFT

EE EE EE EE.

It's his beeper. He glares at his belt. His lips turn downward.

"I'm sorry. I have to run out." He shakes his head and stands up, distracted. "But it seems you have a good take on this. Remember: aside from the tinnitus, the symptoms you described to your friend's father are consistent with panic attacks. And as far as the tinnitus goes, I understand you're a rock musician?" He laughs again, not waiting for me to answer. "No big mystery there, right?" He gives me a last perfunctory smile and shuts the door on his way out.

Fraud

Well. Alone again.

At least my situation isn't so dire as I imagined. A few more questions have been answered. Still, a Pandora's box has also just been sprung. What did he mean by counseling? Am I going to have to start seeing a shrink? Not that I mind. I'm actually relieved at the prospect.

One comic detail: during that brief chat with Dr. Webb, I was still clutching the photo of Mark, Nikki, and me. I hadn't even realized it.

I wonder what a shrink would have to say about that?

I study the image for a minute.

If you looked at Mark and me, you'd probably think that we were the two best friends in the world, having the time of their lives. And on one level, that's true. But you'd never know that one of us believed he was dying, and that the other had just hired a hooker, and that one is annoyed with the other, and that both are keeping secrets. So on another level, the picture is as fake as it looks. Which means Mark was right. It *belongs* on the walls in my home.

Those walls are a testament to fraud.

I've never really thought about it until now. I mean, I have, but not in the intensive way you think about things when you're alone on a hospital bed. (Billy Rifkin, if you can hear me, I apologize for the thousandth time. I admit: I thought that your little sermon about dying and being reborn sounded corny. I regret that. Because . . . now I'm starting to understand it. A little bit, anyway. Besides, where the hell do I come off judging you? I didn't lose my ability to walk. Compared to you, nothing happened to me.)

Anyway, now I know what my parents believe about those photos. I've known it forever, inside. They believe: photos always tell the truth. Why wouldn't they? They're instantaneous! Naturally they should represent what life is like at its most candid and natural, right?

And they do, on a superficial level.

But in my home, it's all superficiality. There's nothing deeper.

DANiEL EHRENHAFT

The photos represent what life is supposed to be like.

Look at how happy this family is, you might say, examining all our portraits. You might even believe we were super-close. You would. I would! That's the scary part. Because the more time passes, the more truthful the fraud becomes. The memories fade. Only the false representations remain. And soon even I won't be able to tell the difference. I'll brainwash myself into believing that I was happy once, that we all were. I'll think: *Here I am, with my super-close family!*

I won't even remember why I called them out-of-their-gourds wacko. . . .

No wonder I suffered a panic attack.

Cartoon Characters

A few minutes later there's a loud knock on the door.

"Come in," I call.

The door swings open. I was hoping it would be Mark. It's not. It's my parents. They look even more wiped out than he did. Mom clutches her handbag in front of her. The sharp creases in her business suit match the worry lines on her forehead. Dad's in a suit, too—though his is considerably less crisp. His gray hair is uncombed. He looks as if he spent the night sniffing Elmer's in an empty lot.

"How are you, Ted?" he asks, hesitating in the doorway.

I muster a smile. "I've had better days, I guess."

Mom stares down at her feet. "Ted . . . I—I just don't know what to say. I just never . . . This business of the prostitute, of your threatening behavior at the airport, the alcohol . . . This isn't the Ted we know."

I blink. At first my throat tightens. Then I almost laugh. Incredible. *That's* what she has to say to me after everything that's happened? Yes, I screwed up on a variety of levels—but still, I'm their only child, and I'm lying in a hospital bed. And those are the first words out of her mouth? That I'm not the Ted they know?

"But you don't even know me!" I shout.

They both glare at me, aghast.

"Ted!" Dad barks.

"But you *don't*. Listen to you! I was trying to run away! Don't you get it? I mean . . . I'm sorry, but I've been lying here for a while, and I've had a lot of time to think about stuff. Besides, Dr. Webb says I should be allowed to vent because that's why I'm here in the first place. You know, because of the panic attack. Because you guys stress me out. I mean, not *just* you guys, but—"

"Ted!" Dad interrupts, raising his palms and smiling nervously. "Relax, kiddo! Don't get so worked up!"

I sink back against the pillows. "Sorry. But I should feel like I know my own parents. And I don't. You're like these . . . these . . . I don't know—these cartoon characters to me. And I know that sounds harsh, and I know it's partly my fault. But it shouldn't be like that. I mean, yes. Most kids have strained relationships with their parents. But they still have *relationships*. Even Mark, who sees his mother maybe four times a year, even he knows her, deep down—"

"Ted, obviously you're still under sedation," Mom cuts in. "I think we should talk later."

"I think that's a good idea." Dad breathes shakily. "Mark would like to see you again, anyway."

I nod, swallowing. My throat is drier than ever. "Mark is . . ."

Mark's head suddenly floats into view, looming in the doorway between theirs. Boy, do I wish I had that Polaroid now.

"Ted?" Mom says, with the self-possessed tone she always adopts when she's in public.

"Yes?"

"I'm sorry, but . . ." She tries to smile. "I thought of something that might cheer you up. I don't know why—" She sighs and turns away. "A boy named Wes left several messages on our machine. I had a hard time understanding him, but I think he said that if you were still alive, he wanted you to join his band . . . you know, the one you like so much? Chafes the Clown?"

"Really?"

Mark's eyes widen. He bursts into a huge smile. *"Dude!"* he mouths silently.

For some reason, I feel like crying.

Mom and Dad shuffle out into the hall.

"Hey, Mom?" I call after her.

"Yes?"

I clear my throat. "I know I'm not exactly in a position to ask you guys a favor . . . but if Wes calls again, will you do something for me?"

"Yes?"

"Please just tell him no thanks. Tell them I'm starting my own band."

"Will do, kiddo," Dad answers for her.

Walls and Barriers

Mark closes the door behind them.

"I'm proud of you," he says.

I sniff. "Proud?"

"I'm serious!" He steps forward. His hands are clasped behind his back. It looks as if he's hiding something. "I mean, okay, I'm pissed at you, too. But I heard that whole conversation. I heard everything that just went on between you and your parents. And when I heard it, I knew that I was right."

"Right about what?" I mutter, wiped out. I rub my puffy eyes.

"About how Burger was dead."

"Mark," I groan. "Please—"

"No, I *know* you, Ted. You're always trying to impose order on the chaos."

I almost laugh. "Listen, man, I really don't know if I can deal with any sort of grand philosophy right now. I don't need to hear about the doughnut-shaped universe."

"No, no, no! Just let me finish. I do know you. I mean, I knew Burger. See, *Burger* had this weird set of routines and barriers. *Burger* set up all these walls around himself. Which is what I'm talking about. Burger tried to keep things simple, all mellow and whatever, but how could he? There's no way to impose order on the chaos—not even if you let everybody else make decisions for you! Not even if you hide by obsessing about a stupid band all the time! Get it? That Burger is long gone!"

"Mark?"

He closes his wild eyes for a second and then opens them in an exhausted blink. "Yeah?"

"Maybe you should get some rest," I say.

He laughs. "I gotta split right now, anyway. But don't worry. I just got off the phone with Nikki. Rachel's at her place, and they'll be here soon."

I jerk upright. "They're *together*?"

"Yeah. See, Nikki called me as soon as she got home. I

explained what was going on. Then she called Rachel and invited her over to hang out. You know, until they got word that you were all right."

"I don't get it. How did they . . ."

Mark stares at me. "They probably had a lot to talk about. Like how you tried to kiss Nikki in the cab."

I swallow.

"Funny," Mark says. "I don't remember seeing that on the list."

"Mark, I'm so sorry," I blurt. "I swear—"

"Shhh." He raises a finger to his lips. "It was a long time coming."

"But I—"

"Hey, don't think you're so special. We've *all* got walls and barriers. We all run and hide. The good thing is, we've got plenty of time to talk about it now. Right? I mean, just think what Rachel and Nikki are talking about right now."

"I can only imagine."

"Well, don't worry *too* much. We don't want you to have another panic attack. They actually get along really well. They've never really hung out before all that much, you know? Rachel is really, really nice."

I'm at a loss for words again.

"Oh, but before I split, I just wanted you to have this. I wrote it while you were getting examined and stuff, while you were still out. I was gonna give it to the Circle Eat so they could name a meal after you—you know, in a worst-case scenario. It's number ten on the list. It's not a fountain or a park, but whatever. . . ."

Mark shoves another crumpled napkin into my hands and hurries out the door.

THE TED BURGER: Fries and Ketchup on a Bun

$6.95

Named in honor of loyal customer Ted Burger (yes, his real name), who was a big fan of fries. As you enjoy this odd burger, remember that when there *is* no burger, you shed the entire burger identity—and on the last day of his life, Ted Burger learned how to shed the Burger identity, too. That's how he made his mark.

Metaconclusion

Yes, you're entitled to know: A little sniffling goes on.

I blow my nose in the napkin.

Mark Singer is a very wise kid. It's clear, isn't it? He *knows* me. He knows me in the way that only a best friend can.

My whole life, I've fought to impose order on the chaos, to build a wall of routines and barriers. And then came that final day: Burger's spring break, ten things to do before I die, the chapters, the *chapters within chapters*, the visions of my own funeral—the lists, the bullet points, the footnotes . . .

But you *can't* impose order on the chaos. You can't divide it up. Reality isn't like that. Reality isn't neat. It comes as it comes, in a great roar—not in lists and footnotes and chapters, but in real time. There's no way to divide it up, no way to keep it at a safe distance no matter how hard you try. Sure, you can hole up in your room and fantasize about being in your favorite band. Sure, you can pretend that you have a good relationship with a nice, beautiful girl even though you don't. You can even go for years without communicating with your parents; you can even lust after your best friend's girlfriend—and hate yourself for it because you *love* your best friend. . . . But you can't hide. Sooner or later, reality will catch up with you. It always does.

So.

Rachel and Nikki are on their way to see me. *Together.* Mom and Dad are waiting outside to finish the conversation we started. *Together.* A large dose of reality is coming at me. And I'm apprehensive, maybe even a little freaked. But I'm *alive.* I'm not running away anymore. Besides, even if I wanted to run away, I couldn't—because I'm trapped in a hospital bed in Brooklyn.

Honestly, though, I don't want to. Mark was right. Burger is dead. And as far as who takes his place . . . well, I'll just have to wait and see. But I'm hopeful. I really am this time—no joke. The glass is half-full and rising.

DANIEL EHRENHAFT

Epilogue: A Month Later

"I can't believe it," Nikki says.

"What, that we came back here after what happened?"

"No. That they actually added Mark's Ted Burger to the menu."

"Well, of course they did. Who doesn't love fries on a bun?" She laughs.

It's the first time we've been back to the Circle Eat. We're sitting across from each other at our old booth. Looking around, you might think nothing had happened. It still stinks of grease. Nikki is still all in black; I still register a nine-point-five on the Afro Q-Tip meter. Old Meatloaf Lady, Guy with Crumbs in His Beard, P.Y.T.—they've all returned, too, all to their usual counter-stools or tables.

There are two very significant and conspicuous absences, however. Leo is in jail, pending his trial. And where Mark always sat beside Nikki . . . well, my guitar case and her knapsack currently occupy that spot.

"Besides, Mark is a living legend," I add. I glance around. "He saved this place. Speaking of which, he really needs his picture on the wall."

Nikki lays the plastic menu on the table. She stares down at it, her black hair shielding her. "So he didn't want to come today, huh?"

"No, no. He did. It's just he's . . ." I laugh and shake my head. "He's making a documentary about Leo's trial."

Nikki looks up and brushes the black strands out of her face, finally revealing her beautiful, saucer-alien eyes. "Wait—*what?*" she asks, smiling.

"Yeah. He's doing this project with the film club because he's super-pissed that Leo's lawyer isn't pleading insanity. He said that this whole thing jump-started an interest in documentary filmmaking and the legal system. He said that he had a long talk with his father and that he doesn't have a 'thing' either. So he has to find something to do with all his energy. He never had an outlet for it before, and, well, you know, his judgment stinks. . . ." I leave the sentence hanging.

Her smile grows wistful. "So you guys are cool?"

"Getting there." I shake my head, puzzled. "But you know about all this, right? He says he talks to you all the time."

She sighs. "We do talk, I guess. We just don't really . . . you know. *Talk.*"

I nod, looking into the black orbs. I *do* know. And she knows it. Nothing more needs to be said.

"But hey, did you notice the smell when we first came in?" she asks suddenly. "That deep-fried grease smell? It was crazy."

I glance around the diner and lean toward her. "I know exactly what you mean," I whisper so only she can hear. "You know what my shrink told me? Like the very first thing he said to me? I mean, aside from the fact that my parents should probably be in on my sessions, too? He warned me that I shouldn't come back to the Circle Eat. He said that neurological studies prove that odor is the most powerful stimulus for triggering traumatic memories."

"Really?" she asks. "So why *did* you come back here?"

I shrug, settling back in the seat. "Because you wanted to."

"I don't believe you, Ted."

"I'm serious!"

She reaches across the table for my hand. "Don't BS me," she murmurs dryly, looking straight into my eyes.

I laugh. "Okay, I came back here because my band's rehearsal space is right around the corner, and I knew I would be hungry, and the food is good here—*and* I wanted to see you, and I knew you wanted to come here. Satisfied?"

She squeezes my fingers for a moment. "Not really. I think you came back here because you wanted to see your name in print on the menu." Then she lets go and unzips her knapsack.

"You know what I can't believe?" I find myself saying.

"What?" She pulls out a notebook and lays it on the table.

"That you're actually going on that Amnesty International retreat."

She chuckles, clicking open a pen, all business. "Well, I still have to get in first. Rachel said that the spaces are getting really limited. Anyway, it'll probably do me some good to get away this summer. It'll probably do us *all* some good."

I shake my head. "Actually, what I really can't believe is that you guys are so tight now."

Nikki blinks. Her cheeks redden. She concentrates on her notebook. "Neither can I. But you guys are still friends, right? She says she talks to *you*."

"Well, sort of," I reply honestly. "But it's the same thing. We talk, but we don't *talk*. She was so pissed at me that day when you guys came to see me in the hospital. Not that I blame her. She had every reason to be pissed. Basically, every single thing I ever said to her was a lie. Except maybe about Shakes the Clown. She's got a lot of forgiving to do."

"No, she doesn't," Nikki states, still studying her notebook.

I glance at my watch. "She doesn't?"

Nikki shakes her head. "Nope."

"You'll have to tell me why sometime," I say, scooting out of the booth. I want to stay with Nikki and finish this conversation— I want to stay with her no matter where I am or who I'm with— but I have to get to band practice. We're having auditions today for a singer. It's a seminal moment. Once we have a singer, the band will be complete. Finding a bassist and drummer was insanely easy. Mark helped me make a bunch of flyers (nothing offensive, just BASSIST AND DRUMMER WANTED). . . . Anyway, we posted them all over the school, and the bassist and drummer from the jazz band—John and George—answered immediately because as it turns out, Mr. Puccini is friends with the jazz band conductor, who put in a good word for me. The three of us jammed, it clicked, and we've been rehearsing almost every day for the past two weeks. John and George have the same tastes I do. They love Shakes the Clown, too. (The music of Shakes the Clown, that is.) And after we get a singer . . . well, all we have to do is come up with a name. Then it's straight to the Onyx.

"Ted, I'm serious," Nikki says. She grabs my forearm as I reach over her for my guitar. Her ringed fingers are cold against my skin.

"Serious about what?"

"Rachel doesn't have a lot of forgiving to do. She lied to you, too."

I have to laugh. *Very funny*, I think. Rachel is to lying what Pinocchio is to telling the truth. Lying isn't a part of Rachel's makeup. She'd probably have a violent reaction if she tried to tell a lie. She's Honest with a capital *H*. "Uh . . . I think I'm going to have to disagree with you on this one—"

"I mean it, Ted," Nikki says. Her tone softens. Her fingers slide down my wrist to my hand. "She'd kill me if she knew I told you this. But maybe she told me because she *wanted* me to tell you."

My pulse picks up a notch. "Tell me what?" I ask.

"She lied about guitar lessons. She only started taking guitar lessons with Mr. Puccini *after* you introduced yourself to her."

I laugh again. "No, she didn't."

"Yes, she did. She *researched* you, Ted. She had a total crush on you. And when she found out you took guitar lessons from Mr. Puccini, she came up with this huge scheme. She thought that if she just stared and stared at you, you might introduce yourself. And if you did, then she'd already have this Mr. Puccini story in place. And *then* she'd start taking guitar lessons to make the story true. Which is exactly what happened."

I clutch Nikki's hand tightly. "I don't believe you."

"It's true, Ted," she says.

"It's . . ." I let go and glance at my watch again. *Damn.* I'm late. I sling my guitar case over my shoulder. "But if Rachel wanted to meet me, why didn't she just start taking lessons with Mr. Puccini? I mean, before? Wouldn't that have been easier?"

Nikki grins. "Because she's a lot like you, Ted."

"She is?"

"Yeah. She covers up her tortured soul with clownish shenanigans, too. She was worried Mr. Puccini would tell her she had no talent. She was worried about being rejected. By you, by him, by everyone. She was just *worried.* So she came up with a brilliant plan involving staring at you and lying. Make sense?"

I swallow. "No. No, it doesn't."

"Well, don't worry about it too much. She'll get over it. It'll just take time." Nikki smiles briefly and turns back to her notebook. "Anyway, I've gotta write this essay for the retreat. . . ."

DANIEL EHRENHAFT

I lean over to kiss her on the top of the head and then head for the exit. I'm not letting her off the hook. This conversation will *be* finished. She knows it. I know it. We also know we have lots of time. We have an entire future.

"Oh, hey!" she shouts after me. "Who are you auditioning today? You know, for a singer?"

"Billy Rifkin," I call over my shoulder. "Turns out he started taking singing lessons after his accident."